S0-AZP-013

Praise for

A Curious Tale of the In-Between

"DeStefano's vivid prose is both evocative and immersive. . . .
Thematically haunting and skillfully executed, this blend
of ghost story, family drama, and mystery will leave
readers pondering the space between the living and
the spirit world for some time." —*BCCB*

"DeStefano artfully concocts a moving and multilayered tale
that is an effective mix of genres and tones. . . .
Love, loss, and hope are at the heart of this
exciting read." —*Kirkus Reviews*

"Young readers will be forgiven if their blood runs cold
at certain points of Lauren DeStefano's elegant,
disquieting novel." —*The Wall Street Journal*

"The perfect book to hand to readers looking for
the mysterious and spooky." —*Booklist*

"DeStefano creates a beguiling world through haunting
images and descriptions. . . . An eerie, moving story
about 'that murky place between this world and
the one that comes after it.'" —*Publishers Weekly*

"Startlingly dark . . . coupled with a lively paranormal
adventure. . . . Sophisticated readers will appreciate the vivid
characters with rich internal lives." —*School Library Journal*

Books by Lauren DeStefano

A Curious Tale of the In-Between
The Peculiar Night of the Blue Heart

A CURIOUS TALE OF THE IN-BETWEEN

Lauren DeStefano

BLOOMSBURY

NEW YORK   LONDON   OXFORD   NEW DELHI   SYDNEY

Text copyright © 2015 by Lauren DeStefano
Illustrations © by Kevin Keele
All rights reserved. No part of this book may be reproduced or transmitted in any form
or by any means, electronic or mechanical, including photocopying, recording, or by any
information storage and retrieval system, without permission in writing from the publisher.

First published in the United States of America in September 2015
by Bloomsbury Children's Books
Paperback edition published in September 2016
www.bloomsbury.com

Bloomsbury is a registered trademark of Bloomsbury Publishing Plc

For information about permission to reproduce selections from this book, write to
Permissions, Bloomsbury Children's Books, 1385 Broadway, New York, New York 10018
Bloomsbury books may be purchased for business or promotional use. For information on bulk
purchases please contact Macmillan Corporate and Premium Sales Department at
specialmarkets@macmillan.com

The Library of Congress has cataloged the hardcover edition as follows:
DeStefano, Lauren.
A curious tale of the in-between / by Lauren DeStefano.
pages   cm
Summary: Bright, imaginative, eleven-year-old Pram lives with two aunts who run a
retirement home, hiding the fact that she can talk with ghosts—but not the spirit
of her mother—and after befriending Clarence, who also lost his mother, she
decides to find her father in hopes he can answer her questions.
ISBN 978-1-61963-600-2 (hardcover) • ISBN 978-1-61963-601-9 (e-book)
[1. Loss (Psychology)—Fiction. 2. Psychic ability—Fiction. 3. Friendship—Fiction.
4. Ghosts—Fiction. 5. Orphans—Fiction. 6. Aunts—Fiction.] I. Title.
PZ7.D47Cur 2015   [Fic]—dc23   2014035767

ISBN 978-1-61963-602-6 (paperback)

Book design by Amanda Bartlett
Typeset by Westchester Book Composition
Printed and bound in the U.S.A. by Berryville Graphics Inc., Berryville, Virginia
2 4 6 8 10 9 7 5 3 1

All papers used by Bloomsbury Publishing, Inc., are natural, recyclable products
made from wood grown in well-managed forests. The manufacturing processes
conform to the environmental regulations of the country of origin.

*For Riley, who believes in things
before the rest of the world can see them*

Nothing comes to us too soon but sorrow.
—Philip James Bailey

A CURIOUS TALE OF THE IN-BETWEEN

CHAPTER 1

Pram died just before she was born. It was a brutally hot August, and the dogwood tree was parched. Its white blossoms had gone weary and brown without rain. The nurses pitied it. In fact, that was how Pram's mother was discovered. A nurse filled up the janitor's mop bucket with fresh water, and she went outside to water the dogwood tree, as unconventional as that might have been.

Instead, the bucket fell at her feet, and the water spread around the parking lot, never quite reaching the grassy island that contained the tree. For there was a woman hanging by the only branch that looked sturdy enough to support her weight. She was almost too unreal to be a woman at all, if not for her pregnant stomach.

In the next instant, there was a gurney and shears severing the rope, hands easing the woman down with great care as though she could be saved. Pram was inside her, already dead. But doctors aren't put off by the finality of death. They believe it can be negotiated. If they can pull the right strings at the right time, they can make dead things breathe again. So Pram lived after all.

Pram, orphaned right at the start of her life, was inherited by two very practical aunts. They ran the Halfway to Heaven Home for the Ageing out of their two-hundred-year-old colonial house. According to Pram's books, "aging" was misspelled, and Pram noticed only when she first learned to read. She climbed on a chair and scratched the unwanted *e* from the sign with a black crayon and was promptly scolded. The crayon mark was scrubbed down to a dull scar.

Pram wasn't told the story of her birth. But even as a very small girl, she felt deep in her chest that she was alive and dead at the same time.

Pram's aunts had no idea what to do with a little girl, much less how to love one. They did give her the very best things they could think of: a name, for starters. Pram was short for Pragmatic, because after much deliberation, they agreed it was a sensible name for a young lady. It was also a trait her mother had lacked.

They gave her a bedroom in the attic. It overlooked the pond where her mother had liked to swim, and had bright daisy wallpaper, and teddy bears that wore dust hats and dust sweaters. For dessert she was often permitted slices of cake with whole strawberries inside. They gave her a plaid jumper, and Aunt Dee ironed the pleats while Aunt Nan starched the white blouse that went under it. They shined the pennies in her loafers, and they gave her stacks of books to read. Sometimes the books had missing covers or torn pages because they had come secondhand from the charity store in the church or they had been left on the doorstep. It was a small town and everyone knew that Pram liked to read. Before she was six, she had reenacted the great works of Shakespeare with her button-eyed dolls. She would recite Ophelia's final words aloud and pretend to drown herself in the old claw-foot tub.

It was all this reading that made Aunt Dee and Aunt Nan overlook Pram's eccentricities. She was just imaginative. Plus, she entertained the elders. She performed for them, and always with a flair for the dramatic. The elders treated her as a sort of pet, asking her to sit with them and read, brushing her hair, offering her cough drops (as that was the closest thing they had to candy). They shared their watercolors with her during arts and crafts, and asked the aunts to tape her pictures on their bedroom walls.

It wasn't until the boy came around that the aunts began to suspect something was wrong.

Pram first spoke about the boy during an evening bath. She was five at the time.

Aunt Nan dumped a cup of water over Pram's white hair, caramelizing it. "I've made a friend," Pram said. "A boy named Felix."

"Have you?" Aunt Nan said, lathering Pram's hair more roughly than Pram would have preferred. "A grandchild of one of the elders, then?"

"I don't think he is," Pram said.

"Where was he?" Aunt Nan asked.

"In the pond," Pram said.

"In the pond?"

"At first. Then the wind picked up a bit, and the light on the water changed, and he came out of it."

"Is this something you've read about in one of your books?" Aunt Nan asked.

"No," Pram said, scowling as her hair was scrubbed by her aunt's chubby fingers. She could sense that she wasn't going to be believed.

"If you see this boy again," Aunt Nan said, "tell him that pond's not for swimming. It startles the fish."

"What is it for, then?" Pram asked.

"Thought. Out of the tub with you now. It's bedtime."

Pram dutifully performed her evening rituals and climbed into bed.

The attic had one small, circular window that seemed to align with the moon on clear nights. The daisies on her wall had gone silver; the button eyes of her bears and dolls stared with astonishment as the shadows of trees bounced across them.

There was something about trees that made Pram especially sad.

CHAPTER 2

Every September, there came a knock at the front door that carried a certain authority. Pram knew who it was. So did the elders—some of them, at least. The others merely played along when she hid at their feet, thinking this was another of her games.

When the knock came late in the morning, Pram hid under Edgar Frump's wheelchair. It was a gamble, she knew, as Edgar was not especially lucid. But he was closer than the dining room table, which wasn't crowded enough to hide her. The tablecloth had been removed after a prune juice accident just moments before.

"I'm not a doghouse, child," Edgar said. "And you're not a poodle."

"Please," Pram said. "If I'm caught, I'll be taken away. Please."

Edgar straightened his blanket across his legs, hiding her. "Since you said 'please' more than once."

Aunt Nan's steps were thunderous as she came down the hall.

Aunt Dee was lighter on her feet, but she fidgeted. "Of all the mornings," she said. "The house looking the way it does."

Aunt Nan opened the doors of the china cabinet and retrieved the pile of textbooks and notebooks. She hastily spread them on the coffee table, nearly spilling a cup of tea that sat near the edge.

The knock came again, and the aunts stood shoulder-to-shoulder and drew a deep breath in tandem. Pram watched them through a part in the blanket, and in their nervous gestures she could see that they loved her.

The door was opened by Aunt Dee's bony fingers—fingers that went about smoothing her apron an instant later. In came a gust of chilled fall air. Three leaves—a red, a brown, and a spotted yellow—swirled across the scuffed floorboards. The schoolmarm's polished black shoes crushed all of them with their first steps into the house. Pram held her breath.

"Can we fix you some tea?" Aunt Dee said.

"Let me take your coat," Aunt Nan said.

The schoolmarm, Ms. Appleworth, grunted in response. For a woman who taught so many children the English language and put such emphasis on proper enunciation, she spoke very little. The aunts fussed and stumbled as they led her to the coffee table.

"We were just about to sit with Pram for her morning lesson," Aunt Dee said.

"You only give lessons in the morning?" Ms. Appleworth said.

"No, no, lessons all day," Aunt Nan said. "It's toast with jam, lessons, a break for lunch, and lessons until dinnertime."

This was a lie. Pram's lessons were scattered throughout the day. She often did her schoolwork alone by the pond. Sometimes she didn't do it at all; she read things that were not on the lists, things that weren't supposed to be for young girls, things that were frowned upon and long out of print.

"Pram, dear," Aunt Nan called. "Ms. Appleworth is here."

Pram could feel her heart within her ears. She thought it strange that she had one heart capable of filling two ears with noise. She often thought the extra heart belonged to her late mother. She knew that the dead hid pieces of themselves in the world. They buried organs in the living. They stuffed memories into trees and clouds and other innocuous things. It wasn't very often that Pram accompanied her aunts into town, but when she did, she could sense these sorts of things. In shop windows she would see the laughing reflections of the dead. She heard whispers in automobile engines. She could never see these memories clearly, and they disappeared when she blinked, but their existence comforted her. She knew that death was not truly the end and that there was always something left.

"Pram!" Aunt Dee called, a little too hysterically. She cleared her throat. "Don't be shy now."

"Shy?" Ms. Appleworth said. "If she's unaccustomed to visitors, some time in a classroom would do wonders."

The aunts presented a hasty argument. It was guilt and pity that brought Pram out of hiding. She adjusted the pleats of her plaid jumper and hoped it was neat enough to make up for the calamity that was her morning hair.

Ms. Appleworth was as gray as her skirt and vest and hair. She was a drawing that hadn't been colored.

"Hello, Pram," she said.

"Six times twelve is seventy-two," Pram blurted. "I can spell 'arithmetic'; would you like to hear?"

"That won't be necessary," Ms. Appleworth said. "Though I'd be interested to hear about your lessons. Do you enjoy learning?"

This question felt like a trick, and Pram wasn't sure

how to answer. "Sometimes," she said. "When it's something in which I'm interested."

Ms. Appleworth raised her eyebrows. "Most children wouldn't know not to end their sentences in a preposition. How old are you now, dear?"

"Eleven years and twenty-six days," Pram said.

"She's very bright," Aunt Dee said. "She can recite the balcony scene of *Romeo and Juliet* from memory."

Pram would have added that she knew all the multiplication tables, but she could see that it wouldn't matter. Ms. Appleworth was looking at her the way others had looked at her in the past, when they realized she wasn't quite normal.

It was the preposition, Pram thought, angry with herself.

"Thank you, dear," Ms. Appleworth said. "You may run along and do your chores."

Pram didn't have any chores, but she went and collected the breakfast plates and brought a soapbox to the sink so that she could wash them.

Her aunts were having a long discussion with the schoolmarm, and Pram had washed the dishes twice before she heard the front door open and close.

Hands dripping, she walked down the hallway, clenching and unclenching her fists, splashing the walls.

"Boo," Edgar whispered as she passed his wheelchair. He was no longer lucid.

Pram stood before her aunts for a few seconds and then raised her eyes. "I'm sorry," she said. "I tried."

"You haven't done anything to be sorry about," Aunt Dee said, but she was wringing her apron. Aunt Nan was frowning.

"I'll have to go to school," Pram said. "Won't I?"

"For now," Aunt Nan said.

Pram felt sick. "Why?" she asked.

"You're getting older now," Aunt Nan said. "Ms. Appleworth doesn't think it's fair that a girl as bright as you is being taught by the likes of us."

"You're great teachers," Pram said, although she knew that she was being generous. Her aunts could barely keep up with her arithmetic worksheets, and they didn't know the definitions of nearly as many words as Pram did.

Aunt Dee leaned toward Pram and patted her cheek sympathetically. "Ms. Appleworth just wants you to have a good education. That's her job, you know: to make sure that children are getting a good education. You'll start on Monday, and we'll see how it goes."

The air inside the house had grown thin. "I'd like to go outside now," she said.

"Brush your hair first," Aunt Dee said.

"And your teeth," Aunt Nan said.

Pram trudged upstairs, her feet feeling twice as heavy. When she returned downstairs, her aunts presented her with toast and more jam than they'd usually allow. It was the best that they could do.

She wasn't hungry, but she understood the gesture and she ate the whole slice.

Once outside, Pram ran as fast as she could through the fallen leaves. She ran until she reached the pond; she sat at its edge and stared at the green water until her eyes felt heavy with tears.

"The others will make fun of me," she said.

A cloud blocked the sun, then moved away from it, as though playing a game with the light.

"What others?"

Pram wiped at her runny nose. "Felix," she said as the boy sat beside her. "You startled me."

"Why are you crying?" he said.

"I wasn't."

"You were so." He turned his head to the pond and blew, and the reflection of the leaves turned gold. Pram blinked, and they had changed back to normal. She giggled, and Felix smiled with triumph.

"They're making me go to school," Pram said. "I don't think it's a very good idea. I've read about how cruel kids can be."

"Are you afraid they'll be cruel, or that being around them for too long will make you cruel?" Felix said.

"Both, I suppose." Pram touched the pond with the heel of her foot. "Have you ever been to school?"

"No," Felix said. "But I always thought it seemed fun."

"It won't be," she said. "It won't take the other kids long to realize I'm strange."

"I don't think you're strange," Felix said.

Pram fell back into the grass, sighing. "You're a ghost," she said. "You're strange, too."

"A little rude to bring it up like that," Felix said, lying beside her. "I still have feelings."

"I didn't mean it that way," Pram said. "I'm sorry. But don't you see? The other kids will catch me talking to myself and ridicule me."

"You aren't talking to yourself," Felix said, reaching up his arms and arranging his fingers like a picture frame. The clouds took on the shape of dancers; from somewhere far off, Pram heard music before the clouds became normal again.

"But they'd see it that way," she said.

Felix shrugged. "You'll have to be clever and not get caught."

Pram was indeed very clever about not getting caught. In Smith's tailor shop, where Aunt Dee brought their clothes for repair, there was a ghost named Clara; she wore a burgundy dress and a feathered hat. She knew she wasn't alive, but she liked to pretend, twirling about the shop, trying to sell Pram bolts of fabric. She spoke to Pram in English, followed by a prompt translation in French.

While Aunt Dee talked to the tailor, Pram would hide behind the bolts of fabric and play along with Clara, asking to see the silks and for pricing on buttons. But Pram was very careful, and she had never been caught talking to her. And Clara was a mischievous one; she wanted Pram to be caught, just to amuse herself. As it was, Aunt Dee just thought Pram was fascinated by the buttons pinned to the wall there.

Felix was the only ghost that Pram saw every day, though, and therefore it was trickier for Pram to keep him a secret. It did help that her aunts thought he was imaginary; to them she was just a child whose imagination was growing with her.

"Maybe your first day won't be scary," he said. "My first day as a ghost wasn't scary. At least, not that I can remember."

Pram turned her head to him. "You've always told me that you don't remember the day you died."

"That's just it. I don't remember. So how scary could it have been?"

Pram laughed. "I wonder if you were as interesting when you were alive as you are now."

"Don't know," Felix said. "But the spirit world probably changed me. It's quite different here."

"How so?" Pram asked.

"I wouldn't know how to explain it. Just different. You can see more than regular living people can see—me, for instance. But there are other things you'd have to be dead to see."

"Maybe I'll see for myself when I'm old and dead, then," Pram said.

"Don't be in any hurry," Felix said. "I like you alive. I like the way you see things. It makes you who you are, the way the spirit world makes me who I am."

"I like you, too," Pram said.

They watched the clouds for a while, and then, feeling bold, Pram grabbed Felix's hand. His touch was like the ground on a sunny day—she could feel the warmth from where the light had touched him, but beneath that she could feel dead, earthy coldness. She wished he were alive. She wished that when her heart was beating double, she could give one of those hearts to him and then press her ear to his chest and feel it beating.

Across the grassy field, in the two-hundred-year-old colonial, Aunt Dee stood at the window, watching Pram, who lay alone by the pond.

Maybe more time among the living would do the girl some good, she thought.

CHAPTER
3

Monday came, its sky dripping with rain.

"Go on, then," Aunt Nan and Aunt Dee said as the door to the bus yawned open.

Pram had never ridden a bus before, and she found the largeness of the vehicle daunting.

"Haven't got all day, cookie," the woman at the steering wheel said. She was pear shaped.

Hesitantly, Pram boarded the bus. Its floor vibrated from the engine, amplifying her nerves, causing goose bumps. She felt goose bumps only when she was around Felix, mostly, or on the mornings she awoke with an inexplicable chill in her blood and learned at the breakfast table that one of the elders had passed.

The other kids filled all the seats. *They are paper cutouts rather than people,* Pram thought. *They are shadows with black dots for eyes and grim lines for mouths. They almost resemble the dead, but not quite.* It eased Pram's mind to pretend that they were dead—that this was a bus that had crashed somewhere. But most ghosts were friendly, or at least talkative. Like Clara in the tailor shop, and the dead man who wandered the road that led into town, who often forgot he was dead and tried to flag down cars to give him a ride. They realized Pram could hear them, and they had hundreds of years' worth of words for her. None of these children said a word to her.

At the end of a very long, very lonely walk down the aisle, Pram found a vacant seat. There she made herself small against the window, and the bus began to move.

The empty seat at the back of the school bus was like a cold hug. It wasn't kind, but it wasn't unkind, either. It kept her safe and invisible. Pram began seeking more such places once she arrived at the school. She found an empty seat at the back of the classroom, beside the window and in front of the cubbies that held the lunch boxes, which were curtained by soggy raincoats on hooks.

"You're in my seat," a boy said.

His eyes were blue, and so bright they were like an accusation. He was nothing like the gray kids on the bus and in the hallways. He was as alive as could be.

"Your name isn't on it," Pram said with as much

confidence as she could muster. To further assert herself, she raised her chin.

The boy with the blue eyes smirked, and Pram wasn't sure if this was to be a kind smirk or a cruel one. "My name's right there," he said. "Under your hand."

He nodded to her palm, and when she removed it from the desk, she realized that it had been covering the initials *C.B.*

"Clarence Blue," he said.

"Those letters could mean anything," Pram said. "'Courageous Beast,' or 'Crusty Bread.'"

"They stand for 'Clarence Blue,'" he said. "I should know. I'm the one who carved them."

Pram traced her fingertip along the slope of the *C.* "You have nice penmanship," she said.

"Thank you," Clarence said.

The bell rang. It was shrill and it startled Pram.

"Take your seats!" the teacher called from the front of the room.

Pram didn't budge. She had found a spot fair and square, even if someone else's name had been carved into it.

Clarence took the seat beside her, his eyes on her the entire time. She couldn't be sure, but she thought he'd smiled for a moment.

As it would turn out, Clarence always favored the most

hidden seats. During lunch, Pram ran into him when they both happened to approach the last table before the exit, beside the trash bins and under a light that had gone out. Unlike with the school desk, there was room for both of them here.

"After you," he said.

"Thank you," Pram replied.

She opened her lunch box and began unwrapping the slab of strawberry cake her aunts had packed for her lunch.

Clarence raised an eyebrow. "Your mother lets you eat cake for lunch?"

"My mother doesn't let me do anything," Pram said. "She's dead."

Clarence stared at his sandwich. "Oh."

Pram took a fork to her cake, bitter with herself for having said something so strange. Death made people uncomfortable; her aunts had taught her this. The elders made people uncomfortable, too, and that was why they had been left with her aunts to be cared for.

The only ones that made Pram uncomfortable were the living.

"My mother's dead, too," Clarence said.

"Oh," Pram said. "Would you like some cake?" It was too much cake for a small girl to eat alone; her aunts (Aunt Nan in particular) showed their pity with food.

"Yes, please," Clarence said.

Pram severed the cake slice in half with her fork. And as she shared her cake, she wondered why Clarence sought out the shadows the way that she did. He had a face that was just right for making friends. Dozens of friends, if he wanted. To Pram, most of the people in the living world were gray, but Clarence was bright and vivid. In fact, he was the loveliest living thing she'd ever seen. Why would someone like that want to hide?

She couldn't know that Clarence was wondering the same thing about her.

The bell rang, once again startling Pram. She packed up her lunch box and then she stood.

"Wait," Clarence said. "You know my name, but I still don't know yours."

"Pram," she said.

"What about your last name?" he said.

Nobody had ever asked Pram for her last name. She almost didn't remember it. "Bellamy."

"Last names are important," he said. "Last names are older than us. They draw a line way back into our history, further than we can follow it."

"Bellamy" had been her mother's last name, which her mother had shared with her older sisters, Pram's aunts. Pram didn't know her father, but she supposed the line of his family history led into the sea. Her mother had fallen madly in love with a sailor, and that was how Pram was conceived. That was all her aunts had told her of her father. He was a sailor, and he left one day and never returned. He never came to collect his daughter—if he even knew he had a daughter at all.

Pram had been told that her mother died in childbirth, and that it was likely her father never knew about her, and they didn't know how to reach him. Her aunts made up this lie to protect her, and to provide her with closure. They couldn't know the horrible guilt it had given Pram— a guilt that would only increase each year as she grew to appreciate the tragedy of it. She had ended a love affair between a beautiful young woman and a sailor. She felt that, at the very least, she owed her father an apology. And at the very most, she owed him a daughter, if he would have her.

CHAPTER 4

Felix stepped out of the tree's trunk. "How was school?" he said.

"All right," Pram said, searching the grass because she thought she'd seen a ladybug. She didn't see much of them this time of year, so it was a fair guess that it was a ghost. The only way to know the difference between a living insect and a ghostly one was that the ghosts were impossible to catch. She'd cupped her hands around several of them over the years, and when she opened her hands, they would be empty. The insects would reappear on her nose or in her hair. It was a game they played.

"Just all right?" Felix said. "Were the other kids as cruel as you'd thought?"

Pram shook her head. "They didn't even know I was there."

"They clearly weren't looking," Felix said. He couldn't imagine anyone not noticing Pram.

"I like it better that way," Pram said.

"Me, too," Felix said. He stared at the grass. His cheeks were pink. He was quite good at mimicking the living. "I wish we were the only two people in the world," he said.

"Maybe not the only two," Pram said. "There should be some exceptions. My father, for starters."

"Are you still going on about that?" Felix said. "He didn't want you, which means he's a fool."

"He might not know about me," Pram said. "Or he might be angry with me."

"Why would he be angry?" Felix said.

"Because I killed my mother," Pram said.

"If he thinks that, he really is a fool," Felix said.

He frowned to see Pram's glum face. He grabbed the ribbon tied in her hair. With a single pull it came undone, and Pram's white hair opened from its ponytail like it was coming to bloom.

"Hey," she said.

"Want it back?" he said, and ran away.

"Felix!" Pram chased him counterclockwise around the pond, trying to be angry but laughing instead.

He had an unfair advantage over her, being a ghost. He could have disappeared. But he let her catch him. He felt the full weight of her when she crashed into him and knocked him to the ground. He felt her bony knees on his stomach and her hands on his shoulders. She reminded him of what it had been like to be alive.

"Got you," she said, and snatched her ribbon from his fist.

She hopped to her feet and fixed her ponytail while Felix lay in the grass, watching her.

"Pram!" Aunt Dee called from the doorstep. "Come in and wash up for dinner."

"I have to go," Pram told Felix. She didn't even give him a chance to say good-bye before she ran off.

He watched her go. Her ponytail flew behind her like a kite made from a piece of sun.

"Did you have a nice time at school today?" one of the elders—Ms. Pruitt—asked as Pram splashed her cheeks at the kitchen sink.

"It wasn't bad," Pram said.

"I'm teaching advanced watercolors this year," Ms. Pruitt said. "Come to my classroom and I'll teach you everything you need to know."

"I will, Ms. Pruitt," Pram said. Pram knew that the

elders lived in their own imaginary lands. She liked to pretend those imaginary lands were real, though, and that she was surrounded by artists and poets and professional jockeys. It made the house seem magical instead of sad.

At the dinner table that evening, there was minimal fussing from the elders. Aunt Nan, who usually had a scant few minutes to eat her own meal, had to get up only twice, to retrieve a thrown napkin and wipe a dribbly chin.

"Have you made any friends at school?" Aunt Nan asked.

"I don't know if you'd call him a friend," Pram said. "But there was one boy who was nice."

"By this time next year, you'll have a lovely shape," Ms. Pruitt said. "You'll be an early bloomer. I've drawn a lot of ladies, you know."

Pram stared at her plate, blushing.

She'd been worried for some time about growing up. Hanging over the staircase was a black-and-white photo of her mother wearing a polka-dotted swimsuit that overlapped her thighs. She was angelic, with perfectly rolled bangs and a lemon-wedge smile. To go along with the picture, Pram's aunts told her lots of nice stories about her mother. She was the fastest swimmer in her class; she had a good singing voice; she liked reading poetry. It was a lot of pressure for Pram to be her only legacy. She could never hope to be so pretty. Ms. Pruitt might have thought

Pram would have a lovely shape, but she also thought she was an art teacher, and sometimes a radio announcer.

"Is he a handsome boy?" Aunt Dee asked, fixing Edgar's oxygen tank.

"How should I know?" Pram said. "He was a boy, that's all. I don't even remember what he looked like." But she was lying, of course.

"Hmm," Aunt Dee said.

Aunt Nan sighed.

After dinner, Pram went upstairs to have her evening bath. As she reached the last stair, she heard Aunt Dee whisper, "I do hope this boy is real."

CHAPTER 5

The following morning, Pram raced to the desk with C.B.'s initials carved into it. But Clarence had beaten her to it. He sat tall and proud, with his ankle crossed over his knee.

Pram tried not to sulk as she fell into the desk beside his. One of its legs was shorter than the other, and it wobbled when she leaned forward.

"You have to wake up pretty early to beat me," he said.

"Indeed," Pram said.

"But since you shared your cake with me yesterday, I have something for you. Look."

Pram looked where he was pointing. Down and diagonal from his initials, he had carved *P.B.* into the desk.

Pram Bellamy. "I thought we could share it, since we both like sitting here so much," he said.

"Thank you," Pram said. She wanted to hug him, but she thought this would be too strange.

Every day for the next week, they sat together at lunch in the usual spot. The pity of Pram's aunts had worn out by Tuesday, and instead of cake for lunch, they had given her a peanut butter and banana sandwich. Pram nibbled it slowly, careful not to let any of it stick to her teeth.

"I was thinking about what you said last week," Clarence said. "About your mother."

"I said only that she died," Pram said, biting into her sandwich.

"Right. There's a woman in town who can contact her. I haven't been to her myself, but I see flyers on light posts all over, so she must be good."

Pram considered this as she chewed, ever worrying about the peanut butter sticking to her teeth.

Her silence concerned Clarence. "I shouldn't have said anything," he said. "I'm sorry. Forget it."

"She might be fake," Pram said. "If she can speak to the dead, I'd think she'd want to keep it a secret." Pram had never met another person who she believed could talk to ghosts. But she had seen several posters in town for spiritualists, and she'd heard radio ads with howling-wind sound effects and metallic thunder—all fakes, she suspected.

People would pay good money to have access to the dead, and so it was a thriving business. Pram found it detestable that anyone would prey on such a cruel hope.

"Maybe," Clarence agreed. "It's just . . ." He trailed off.

"What?" Pram said.

He shook his head and gnawed pensively on his straw. She stared at him until he answered.

"My mother died last October," he said. "And since then, things have been disappearing from one place and reappearing in another. Some mornings when I wake up, the curtains are drawn. She used to do that to get me out of bed. I wonder if I'm being haunted."

He probably wasn't being haunted, Pram thought. Objects like curtains and hairbrushes and things failed to hold the interest of ghosts. Although Pram did recall having an argument with Felix once and going to bed only to discover one of her stuffed bears had been hidden.

Mostly, though, grief made people misplace things. She'd seen it happen to the elders, and to her, when she was thinking about her father. She might forget to cap the toothpaste or set her shoes in a different place because her mind was elsewhere.

"She'll cost money," Pram said.

"I've got that," Clarence said.

Pram took another bite of her sandwich and swallowed hard. "Okay," she said. "When?"

"Friday. We can go there after school."

"I'll have to ask my aunts," she said, though she didn't think it would be a problem. They would be happy she'd made a friend.

"I can introduce myself," he said.

"Good idea," she said. They might believe he was imaginary otherwise, the way they believed Felix was imaginary.

On Friday, Clarence rode home with Pram on the bus. He didn't have to ask her which seat she preferred; he went straight to the back and let her take the seat by the window. They didn't talk, and Pram wondered if he'd noticed her hair. That morning, Aunt Dee had walked in on Pram's clumsy attempt at a braid, and with a sympathetic laugh, she'd fixed it into two perfectly braided pigtails with mismatched ribbons.

She spotted Felix as the bus drove past the pond. He was swinging from a tree branch and propelling himself into the water. For months he'd been trying to get her to climb with him, but she'd refused.

Clarence followed her gaze to the pond. "What are you staring at?" he asked.

"Nothing," she said.

"Nothing at all?"

"No."

They got off the bus and didn't talk during most of the short walk to Pram's house. It was a chilly September day, and Pram knew that if she were to touch Felix's skin, it would be chilly as well. But she wondered what it would be like to touch a living boy—if he'd be warmer.

"Where do you live?" Clarence asked.

"In that house over there," Pram said, nodding ahead. Hers was the only house in sight, with crumbling white paint and a rusted red star on the front door.

"'Aging' is spelled wrong," Clarence said.

"I know."

They climbed the front steps, and Pram pushed open the front door and said, "I'm home! I've brought the boy I told you about." She hesitated to say "friend" because that was a powerful word, and she didn't want to scare him off.

"Hello," he said to the room of milling elders, who paid them no mind. He had no way of knowing that none of the female elders were Pram's aunts. For all he knew, she lived among them, caring for them as a sort of youthful queen.

Aunt Nan came out of the kitchen, wringing her hands on a dishcloth. "So you did," she said excitedly. "Dee, Pram's brought home a friend."

Pram waited nervously to see if Clarence would object to being called her friend. He didn't.

Aunt Dee bounded down the stairs, trying in vain to smooth her hair back against its gray bun. "I see that," she said, grinning like a madwoman. "Hello, welcome, would you like something to eat?"

"We aren't staying," Pram said. "We're going to walk into town."

The smile faded from Aunt Dee's face. "Town? What for?"

"To see a show," Clarence said smoothly. It wasn't a lie; the spiritualist was performing a show, which was one of the many reasons Pram thought she was a fake.

"It'll be dark soon," Aunt Nan said.

"My father will drive us home. He'll be off from work by then," Clarence said. "I could give you his phone number if you'd like."

Pram's aunts looked at each other, clearly taken aback by this boy who spoke so politely. They had raised Pram to be just as polite, but they functioned under the belief that other children were about as formal as wolves. They couldn't decide if this level of politeness made them feel delighted or nervous.

Aunt Dee handed Clarence a blank recipe card and the pen they used to write down phone messages.

"Edmund Blue," he wrote in the practiced handwriting Pram admired. Below that, he wrote his father's phone number.

"'Edmund Blue,'" Aunt Nan read aloud. "Not the one who owns the refinery?"

"The very same," Clarence said.

Pram didn't know what was so remarkable about the refinery or why it mattered who owned it.

"Be back by six thirty," Aunt Dee said. "We'll keep dinner warm for you."

"Okay," Pram said.

Once she and Clarence were outside, she glanced back at her aunts, who were huddled together behind the window, watching her.

"How did they know about your father?" she asked.

"It's nothing," Clarence said. "Forget it."

As they walked into the horizon, they passed Felix, who was hiding in the pond despite Pram's warning that it wasn't for swimming. And Pram couldn't know the fuss her new friend had caused at the house. She couldn't know that Clarence Blue was the son of the wealthiest man for miles.

They walked for half a mile, until the sidewalk turned to a cobblestone path, lit up by the windows of tiny shops. Pram stopped to admire a mannequin adorned in lace and stripes in the dress shop window. Clarence watched her, thinking there was something magical about the way that most ordinary light touched her face.

He didn't know how to tell her this, so he bought

ice-cream cones from a cart that was just about to close. The man in the striped shirt charged him only half price because it was the end of the day.

Pram thought the chocolate-raspberry swirl was heavenly. But all she said were "Thank you" and "Where are we going?"

"Around the block," Clarence said. "I've been by it a few times, but I was never brave enough to go inside. I'd have needed tickets anyway."

"Can I see the tickets?" Pram asked, biting into her ice-cream cone to hear it crunch.

Clarence reached into his shirt pocket and retrieved the tickets. Though they were brand-new, the coloring made them look like antiques, Pram thought. People took more stock in things that were old. LADY SAVANT'S SPIRIT SHOW—ADMIT ONE was printed on each ticket.

"Clarence," she said, and paused as she thought of a delicate way to word things. "What is it you're hoping Lady Savant can tell you?"

Clarence sat on a bench, and Pram sat beside him. "My mother died in a car accident," he said. "The doctors said that it happened in an instant. I suppose all I want is a chance to say good-bye. That's it."

"There used to be an elder back at the house," Pram said. "It must have been one, maybe two years ago. All she ever said was good-bye. You'd bring her the morning tea, and she'd nod and say good-bye. You'd tell her it was time for her bath, and she'd grab her walker and inch toward the bathroom and say good-bye. I would wonder why that was all she said."

"What happened to her?" Clarence said.

"She died in her sleep," Pram said. "And after, she had children and grandchildren who came by to collect the last of her things. They asked my aunts if she had been in any pain in her last days and what her last words had been. And my aunt Nan told them that her last word had been the same word she'd said every day for weeks: 'good-bye.' I hadn't understood it until then. I suppose she knew that any moment could be her last, and when her family came asking about her, they would know that she had told them good-bye. It's a small word, but it means a lot, doesn't it?"

Clarence nodded. "That's a sad story," he said. "But I like it. Not a lot of people get the chance to say good-bye. I guess she knew that."

"Yes," Pram said. "But it is a sad way to live, always thinking about the end."

"I don't think my mother ever thought about the end," Clarence said. "I bet she thought she was going to live for a hundred years. I thought she would."

"I'm sure that she was wonderful," Pram said.

As Pram finished her ice-cream cone, Clarence offered

her a napkin. He didn't tell her about the raspberry smudge on her nose, partly to be polite, but mostly because he found it charming.

After she threw her napkin into the trash, he said, "Shall we?" He offered his arm, and she hooked her elbow around his.

"We shall," she said cordially.

They might have missed the entrance to Lady Savant's Spirit Show if not for the poster at the mouth of the alleyway. Pram had been in town frequently, but never down its alleys. She didn't know there was anything in them besides trash bins and maybe some rats.

Clarence mistook Pram's hesitation for fear. But really she was looking at the open doorway in the alley. It was a rectangle of yellow light, and from where she stood Pram could smell the incense. There was a man standing by the light, and Pram couldn't tell if he was living or a ghost. Rarely did she struggle to tell the difference. She could usually tell right away when she was dealing with a ghost. Ghosts looked just like the living, and they even moved as though they were breathing. But there was a certain energy they carried, an urgency to be somewhere that no longer existed, or to do something that could no longer be done.

But this man, while he appeared to be living, did not seem entirely present. That would be one way to tell if

Lady Savant was for real. She could ask Clarence if he saw the man, but if he didn't, he would know immediately that she was strange.

Or maybe he already knew. He was staring at her.

"Sorry," she said.

"Are you frightened?" he said.

"No," Pram said, and stepped forward, tugging him with her.

"Tickets," the man at the doorway said. Pram was greatly relieved.

Clarence presented their tickets and they entered, still arm in arm. Now it was Clarence who felt nervous. He'd worn his nicest button-down shirt today, and spent extra time at the mirror brushing his chestnut-brown curls, all in the hope that his mother would be pleased with his appearance. She had been an elegant woman who cared greatly about such things.

Pram had given up any hope of meeting her own mother. She'd thought about it, of course—especially when Felix came along, and on the third Sunday of each month, when she and her aunts left flowers at her gravestone. But there was no trace of her mother anywhere. Sometimes the dead had no reason to linger in the living world.

She once asked Felix if he had known her mother or her father, since he'd been at the tree for so many years.

He told her that he remembered a woman splashing about in his pond. Maybe there had been a man with her sometimes; he really couldn't be expected to have kept track. Time did not pass in the same way for the dead as it did for the living. Pram's mother and father might as well have existed a million years ago, for all he cared. Pram was the only living thing he cared about, and it was because she was the only living thing who cared about him, too.

She could see that Clarence was uneasy. "Here," she said, and pushed away one of the curls that had tumbled over his forehead.

He smiled gratefully.

The room was small and crowded. Most of the folding chairs were already full. There were some empty seats in the back, but this was one time Clarence didn't want to hide. He grabbed a chair from the back and dragged it closer to the stage, and Pram did the same.

In moving the chairs, they had to let go of each other's arms, and they both felt a peculiar chill now.

Pram craned her neck and studied the crowd. They all appeared to be living. They were holding each other's hands and talking; many of them were sobbing. A ghost wouldn't think to occupy a chair—like the living, ghosts don't care to be sat upon. A ghost would also know to look for someone like Pram; Felix had told her that she buzzed like an electric fence.

Though the lights were already dim, they dimmed further. The makeshift curtains at the stage (bedsheets, most likely) swished. The man standing at the door called out, "Silence, please, as Lady Savant approaches."

Pram didn't understand the need for the theatrics.

The sheets/curtains parted, and from them emerged Lady Savant. She was a short, pudgy woman. Her arms were covered in bracelets, and rings sat on her fingers like bejeweled insects. Her hair was in a beehive, and one of her false lashes had come halfway unglued. Pram could see that she was a young woman under all that makeup.

She didn't welcome her audience. She didn't address them at all, except to raise one finger to the crowd and say, "Shh!"

She sat upon the wooden crate that had been placed on the stage and closed her eyes.

"My heart is heavy this evening," she said. "Someone here has lost a loved one to an act of great sadness."

Clarence tensed. Pram looked at him, but his eyes were glued to Lady Savant, the reflection of her jewels in his eyes.

"A car accident?" one woman called out.

"A diving mishap?" gasped another.

Lady Savant shook her head furiously, and at last she opened her eyes. "It was a broken heart," she said.

Pram was still looking at Clarence and didn't notice

right away that Lady Savant was looking right at her until Clarence nudged her.

"You," Lady Savant said. "Did you come here to find someone you've lost?"

"Me?" Pram said, feeling uncomfortable to have so many pairs of eyes on her. Everyone in the room was staring. "I just came with a friend."

"But is there anyone who could be looking for you?" Lady Savant said, her voice a theatrical whisper. "Someone who took her own life?"

"I'm sure there isn't," Pram said.

"Could it be *my* mother?" Clarence said. "She died in an accident."

"Perhaps," Lady Savant said. "Was she very sad when she died?"

"Yes," Clarence said.

"Could the accident have been on purpose?" Lady Savant said. "A suicide."

What an absurd question, Pram thought. An accident happening on purpose.

"No," Clarence said. "I'm very sure."

"This woman is looking for her young daughter so she can apologize," Lady Savant said. She looked at Pram again. "Are you certain your mother isn't looking for you?"

"Yes," Pram said. She didn't know many things about her mother, but she knew that if her mother's ghost were to visit, the last thing it would want to do is apologize. Pram thought that her mother's spirit had moved on. Wherever she was now, she must have had no use for a living daughter.

"Then this spirit is not your mother."

Lady Savant turned back to the crowd, this time channeling a man who'd died in the war. No fewer than five women took interest in this spirit.

Clarence stared at his lap, and Pram ached for him. She didn't say "I told you so," which Clarence appreciated greatly because she could have.

They were both quiet for the remainder of the show.

Once it was through, Clarence called his father from a pay phone to collect them. It was dark now, and most of the shop windows had gone black.

Clarence hung up the phone and joined Pram on a bench under a street lamp. She was swinging her feet and staring at her shoes. They were well-polished loafers with a heart-shaped leather pocket that housed a penny in each shoe.

"I'm sorry," she said.

"Never mind," Clarence said. "It was silly of me to have expected anything."

"I meant that your mother was sad when she died," Pram said. "I'm sorry about that."

Clarence looked at her. She had since become aware

of the raspberry smudge on her nose and wiped it away. No matter. She had a small, pert nose, and it was pretty either way.

"Was your mother sad?" he asked.

"I don't know," Pram said. "All I know is that she had light hair and freckles, and she liked to swim."

Clarence had spent nearly a year in the grayness of grief, studying the misplacement of objects and looking for signs of his dead mother. He hadn't given any thought at all to the living. He'd hidden from life, forgotten his friends, and isolated himself from their symposium of card games, insects, and other simple pleasures that all seemed equally meaningless.

Until Pram came along and took his seat. And when he'd learned that she was also motherless, he'd thought they could share their grief the way they shared that desk. But Pram didn't seem to be grieving. She appeared to be incomplete in some other, more mysterious way.

"What's it like to be able to remember someone you lost?" Pram asked him. She had lost both of her parents before she was born.

"It's like my mother has become an actress in a play," Clarence said. "And the play isn't told in order, and sometimes the lines have changed. Sometimes I'm sitting too far away to see her face or hear her voice."

"What's the play about?" Pram asked.

"It's all just moments she's lived before," Clarence said. "Good ones, mostly. Like how she had a silk scarf wrapped around her neck, and when she drove with the top down in the car, it flew behind her, and the way it fluttered it looked like the entire world was underwater."

"That sounds wonderful," Pram said. It was a proper memory, unlike the black-and-white photo of her own mother that hung over the stairs.

"It is, sometimes," Clarence said. "But then, just when it starts to feel real, it disappears."

Pram could feel the sadness in his words. Although Clarence was a living boy, sometimes she could sense him just as well as she could sense ghosts. It boggled and intrigued her, and she wondered if it was normal for one living person to be so attuned to another.

"Tomorrow is Saturday," Clarence said. "We could do something else, if you'd like. My father will have one of his drivers take us anywhere we want to go."

Pram raised her head. The street lamp placed a halo of light in her hair. "Do you like the ocean?" she said.

CHAPTER
6

Every Saturday for the next several weeks, Clarence's driver brought them to the ocean. Pram wore a heavy sweater and sat on a towel, watching the boats leave the docks. Clarence sat beside her and scanned the newspapers for new spiritualists. Whenever he found a promising lead, Pram accompanied him. Sometimes she saw ghosts and other times she didn't, but none of the spiritualists ever noticed them.

Clarence became increasingly sullen, and Pram worried for him. She was beginning to wonder if she should tell him about the things that made her strange. But she worried that her inability to find his mother would anger him. He might not understand that she couldn't control which ghosts appeared. He might not understand that most people never became ghosts at all.

Her worry made her less talkative. Clarence noticed and thought he had done something wrong.

On Sunday afternoon, after a morning confined by the dreary stained-glass windows of the cathedral, Clarence made the half-mile walk to Pram's house so he could apologize.

He spotted her from the road. She sat by the pond near her house, plucking at blades of grass. He stood and watched her. She was talking to herself, and sometimes she paused and then laughed as though she was having a conversation. Clarence spoke to himself sometimes, but this was different. She seemed to be asking questions and receiving answers from the wind.

It was early November now, and he could see that her ears had turned red from the cold.

Pram didn't notice him. She was too distracted by Felix, who swung from a branch over her head.

"I wish you'd come down," she said.

"Does your boyfriend climb trees?" he teased.

"He isn't my boyfriend," Pram said. "And no."

Felix jumped down and knelt in front of her. "You aren't yourself today," he said. "You haven't been yourself for weeks, and you hardly come and play with me anymore."

"I've had a lot of thinking to do," Pram said. "I may be about to make a big decision."

Felix looked concerned. "What is it?" he said.

"I may tell Clarence that I can see ghosts."

"You can't!" Felix said. "He'd tell the authorities, and you'd be sent away to the circus. Or there are worse places, you know!"

He was being serious, but Pram couldn't help giggling. "I don't think that will happen," she said. She leaned back on her elbows, still giggling. Felix was stoic. "Oh, come on," she said, reaching for one of his hands and pulling him down beside her.

"Be careful, Pram," he said. He lay back in the grass and bumped his head against her shoulder.

She threw bits of grass into the air like confetti. "Aunt Dee says I'm very pragmatic," she said.

"Maybe you could tell him another secret. A smaller one, to test whether he's trustworthy."

"Like what?" Pram asked.

"Tell him what your hair looks like in the morning. If that doesn't scare him off, nothing else will."

"Felix, that's mean." But she laughed.

Felix smiled, but that smile faded when he saw Clarence watching them from the road. He stood, braced himself, and jumped into the pond. Pram would have called after him, but now she saw Clarence.

How long had he been standing there?

She waved, and he started walking toward her. His hands were in his pockets, and he looked handsome in his Sunday suit.

Pram stood to meet him and dusted the grass from her wool coat and her skirt. "Hi," she said. "What are you doing here?"

"I came to see you," he said. "Were you just talking to someone?"

Ripples appeared on the pond that weren't entirely the wind's fault.

Pram didn't want to lie. She was particularly bad at it, and it gave her a stomachache. She was good at changing the subject, though. "I'm glad you're here," she said. "There's something I wanted to show you."

She grabbed his hand and led him back to the house. Halfway there, they turned their walk into a race and started running. Clarence would have let her win, but he didn't have to. She was brimming with energy. She waited for him on the front steps, but once he'd caught up, she ran inside and raced him up the stairs.

Aunt Nan stood in the kitchen, cringing as the children's footsteps pounded through the house. But she didn't have the heart to scold them.

"Bulls in a china shop," Ms. Pruitt muttered into her water cracker.

"That little girl thinks I'm a house," Edgar said as Aunt Dee fixed his blanket.

Aunt Dee knew this to be his usual nonsense. "Don't break anything!" she called after the children. But she was smiling.

Pram doubled over in the doorway of her attic bedroom to catch her breath. Clarence caught up to her and clutched the frame. He used to run before his mother died. He'd forgotten, and Pram had made him remember.

Pram fixed her ponytail. There were bits of grass in her hair. When she looked at Clarence again, her eyes were wide and very serious. "I'm trusting you with a big secret," she said. "I've never told anyone, and you can't, either."

"I promise," Clarence said. "Promise" was too small a word. Pram thought so, too, and she held her fist to him, pinkie extended. He linked his pinkie around hers, and with a firm shake, the promise was official.

She led him across her room, past a cabinet of stuffed bears, and into a closet with a wedge-shaped door. Once he'd followed her inside, she closed the door behind them and pulled the cord that turned on the light.

She knelt on the ground and pulled up the small floral mat that lay there. "This used to be my mother's room, a long time ago," Pram said. She ran her fingers over the floorboards until she found the one that was loose. She pried it up, revealing a rectangle of darkness that looked like a missing tooth in the floorboards. Clarence felt uneasy as he watched her reach into that darkness; there might be mice.

But all she retrieved was an old shoe box and a sheet of dust, which she brushed away with a small cough.

He knelt beside her. "What is it?" he asked.

"Lower your voice," she whispered. "I found it one day when I was looking for my teddy bear." Felix had taken the bear after she'd made him angry, but she didn't tell Clarence that. "It's some of my mother's things. She must've hidden them from her sisters."

Pram methodically unpacked the contents of the box. There were black-and-white photographs of a handsome young man who, Clarence thought, had Pram's heavy eyelids and timid smile. He was the subject of every photo, with the ocean a white-and-silver swirl behind him.

There was also a stack of letters, bundled together by twine, and a compass. At the very bottom of the box was a postcard. Pram held it up between her middle and index fingers.

Clarence leaned close so that he could read it.

Lily,

I see your exquisite face at every port. I've made a horrible mistake leaving you behind. Forgive me, forgive me, forgive me.

Max

"Max is the man in all the letters," Pram said. "I think he's my father. Maxwell Baines."

"Where is he now?" Clarence said.

Pram shrugged. "Around. None of the envelopes have a return address. And the postmarks are all smudged away, so I don't know when they stopped seeing each other, but I'm not mentioned in any of them."

"Maybe your mother didn't tell him about you," Clarence said. He couldn't imagine the willpower it would take to keep a secret as enormous as a child. Pram was very secretive about things, though, so he supposed it was possible her mother had been the same way.

"Maybe not," Pram said. She placed everything neatly back into the box. "They were very in love, though, and he must miss her horribly. The letters say that my aunts didn't like him. They met one summer, and when he came to visit her after that, my mother kept it a secret from them."

Clarence watched as she replaced the box and the floral mat.

"I want to look for my father," she said. She wanted to also tell him about Felix, who hated the idea of her searching for her father. She wanted to tell Clarence all about the ghosts. But this was a safer secret, she thought. And if he kept it, she would be able to trust him with Felix later, when she'd worked up enough nerve to tell him.

"When?" Clarence said.

"I was going to wait until I was older," Pram said. "But . . ."

She was quiet for a long time.

"What?" Clarence asked.

She stared at her lap. "I thought you might want to help me look for him. The way we've been looking for your mother."

"But your father isn't dead," Clarence pointed out. "We wouldn't be employing spiritualists."

"That's exactly my point," Pram said. "He's alive somewhere. It would just be a matter of getting to him."

Clarence was finding it difficult not to take offense. He stood and opened the closet door.

"Where are you going?" Pram asked.

"Home," he said.

"Wait," Pram said. "I didn't mean to upset you."

"I don't understand why you'd want to find him at

all," Clarence said. "He's a stranger to you." His mother wasn't a stranger; couldn't she be a priority? Being dead didn't make her less important. He had expected Pram to understand that, but perhaps he'd been wrong about her.

"That's just it," Pram said. "He may not even know about me. I'd just like to find out."

Clarence walked to the door. Pram followed him halfway across her bedroom.

"Please don't go," she said.

He paused in the doorway, his back to her. He clenched his fists in his pockets, and then he walked away.

CHAPTER 7

Felix was not fond of Clarence.

Shortly after Clarence left, Pram sat at the pond's edge, heartbroken because of that boy. It had taken her so long to make a living friend, and he'd hurt her.

Felix petted her hair. "Don't be sad," he said. "Thank goodness you didn't tell him about your ability to see me, if that's how he handles things. He would have gotten you sent to the circus for sure."

"No, he wouldn't," Pram said. "I was rude. I made it sound like finding my father was more important than finding his mother's ghost."

"You'd have found her by now if she wanted to be found," Felix said.

Felix never left the property, but she didn't point this out.

"I should apologize," Pram said.

"He should apologize," Felix said. "You shared that big secret with him, and he stormed off."

"Well, whether he wants to help me or not, I'm going to look for my father," Pram said. "I've decided that it's time."

"I'll go with you," Felix said. He didn't like the idea of Pram embarking on such a venture alone.

"Really?" Pram said. He never left the pond.

"Where should we start?"

"I've been watching the sailors leave the docks," Pram said. "Every Saturday, I try to get the courage to ask if any of them know my father. I'm afraid they'll laugh at me. Adults laugh at children all the time."

"When should we go?" Felix asked.

"I don't know," Pram said. "Tomorrow, maybe."

"Tomorrow sounds fine," Felix said.

Neither of them wanted to admit being frightened.

That night in bed, Pram lay awake and considered Clarence's question about wanting to find her father. She didn't have an answer, and perhaps that absence of an answer *was* her answer. If she wanted to imagine her mother, she had the photo that hung over the stairs. But if she wanted to imagine her father, she had nothing. He was a shadow.

She could look in the mirror and see her mother, a little, if she didn't smile too much. But the rest of her was unaccounted for.

She wished she knew how to explain this to Clarence. He knew both of his parents. When he sought his mother's ghost, he knew what he was looking for. But in searching for her father, more than anything Pram was searching for a bit more of herself.

The next day, Clarence remembered that it was Pram's turn to have the desk. He didn't say anything as she sat beside him.

"Are you still angry?" she said.

He couldn't stay angry, so he said, "No."

"Good," she said. "I snuck two cookies into my lunch box."

"What kind?" he asked.

"Chocolate chip."

The bell rang and lessons began.

During lunch, Pram and Clarence ignored their sandwiches and ate the cookies instead.

"So all those times we went to the beach," Clarence began, "was that because you wanted to look for your father?"

Pram nodded.

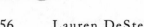

"You could have told me."

"I thought you'd find me strange," Pram said.

Clarence laughed. "I've dragged you to every spiritualist in the city, and you thought I'd find you strange?"

"Everyone else does," Pram said. "My aunts tell me I ought to be careful about the things I say."

"Well, I don't," he said. "Is finding your father what you really want?"

"It really is," Pram said confidently.

"What if—" Clarence paused, like he was trying to find a way to be tactful. "Well, what exactly are you expecting when you find him? You said that he's a sailor. What if he lives on the ocean?"

"I think living on the ocean might be fun." Pram shrugged. "If he wanted me, I'd like to travel with him. But if he doesn't, that's okay, too, I suppose. Really, I just want to know for sure."

Clarence nodded. "I'll help you."

"Really?" she said.

"It's what friends do," he said. "I should know. I used to have plenty of them once."

They must not have been very good friends if they weren't still around, Pram thought. But she didn't know much about having friends.

As she ate the last of her cookie, she became overcome with guilt. If Clarence was going to help her with the great task of finding her father, she should do all that she could to help him find his mother.

"Friends shouldn't keep secrets, should they?" Pram said.

Clarence felt a spark of delight to think she was finally opening up to him. "They shouldn't," he agreed.

"Come home with me after school," she said. "There's someone I'd like you to meet."

Once they got off the school bus, Clarence wasn't surprised that Pram led him to the pond. He'd seen her talking to someone there yesterday. Even though he hadn't seen anyone with her, he was sure she hadn't been alone.

It was a chilly afternoon, and Pram rubbed her gloved hands together. She was nervous. She'd never introduced anyone to Felix before—not since she realized she was the only one who could see him. She wasn't entirely sure how this would work.

The tree branches shook on the wind. There were few leaves left clinging to them, and they shivered like paper bells.

Felix stood below them, arms crossed, scowling.

"Don't be angry," Pram said. "I've brought Clarence because he's my friend, and he'd like to be yours, too."

"Who are you talking to?" Clarence said.

"Felix," Pram said. "He's a ghost."

Clarence stared at the empty space below the tree. "Oh," he said. "Are you sure?"

Pram laughed. "Very," she said. "He's in a mood today."

Felix dived backward into the pond. The splash was extraordinary, but Clarence didn't see it. Felix was in charge of whether or not the living could see his tricks. Any other schoolboy would have doubted Pram at this moment. Seeing ghosts wasn't a common talent, and young girls were known for their imaginations. But Clarence had come to know Pram in the time they'd spent together, and he believed her.

"Felix," she said to the pond crossly. "Please come out of there."

Felix bobbed to the surface. "What does it matter?" he said. "Your boyfriend can't see me."

Pram's face turned red. "He isn't—he's not—just let him know you're here."

Clarence waited with more patience than Pram, who was fidgeting. But then her face broke into a smile and she pointed to the sky. "Clarence, look," she said.

In the fall sky, the clouds shifted and took on the shapes of ballroom dancers twirling about.

Clarence was astonished. "You're doing that?" he said.

"Felix is."

The scene melted back into clouds. An ill-timed blink, and Clarence might have missed it entirely.

"Shall I sing and dance for you as well, Your Highness?" Felix grumbled.

Pram looked overhead to where he was sitting in the tree. "Thank you," she said. When she smiled, he found it hard to stay angry, but he didn't want to admit it, and so he disappeared from sight.

Clarence looked at the clouds as though they might perform for him again. He wasn't very surprised that they had danced. There was something about Pram; when he was with her, he felt that anything was possible.

"Why didn't you tell me sooner?" Clarence said.

"I didn't know how you'd react," Pram said. She sat in the grass with her legs folded, and she smoothed her skirt pleats. "Felix says that people like me get sent off to the circus if they're found out."

This hadn't occurred to Clarence, but now that he thought about it, the circus did seem to be a home for people with surreal talents.

He sat next to her. He stared at her bare knee, admiring the fine blond hairs that glinted in the sun. He didn't see the ghost ladybug that she saw flutter and land there.

"I also thought you would be angry because I couldn't

help you find your mother," Pram said. "Sometimes people don't become ghosts. Sometimes they just move on."

"Where do they go?" Clarence asked.

"I don't know." Pram shrugged. "Just . . . on. I used to look for my own mother, but she's never answered me. She's moved on, and maybe that's a good thing. Maybe she's happier wherever she is and she wouldn't want me to come find her." She looked at him, sympathetic. "It doesn't mean we have to stop looking for your mother," she said. "Maybe she's still hiding somewhere."

"She wouldn't hide from me," Clarence said. "She might hide from my father; she was angry with him for being gone most of the time."

He looked up at the clouds, and so did Pram.

Even though Pram hadn't asked him to, Felix made the clouds dance again.

CHAPTER
8

After school the following day, Pram visited Clarence's house for the first time. It was a majestic Tudor house surrounded by gardens that had gone to sleep until the springtime. Stone gnomes and angels filled the gardens, and it seemed that they were also sleeping, as though a witch had cast a spell on them.

Pram thought a dozen people could have lived in that house and still not have filled all its rooms. But no one was home, aside from a woman in a black dress and white apron, who took their coats and offered them crackers and tea.

"No, thank you," Clarence said. "We'll be upstairs."

The staircase was thrice as wide as any Pram had ever seen. Even the banister was extra thick.

"Who else lives here?" she asked.

"Just my father and me," Clarence said. When they reached the top of the staircase, he said, "My mother's room is that one." He nodded to the only door that wasn't brown. It was painted light blue, with the chipped silhouette of a bird in the center, its beak open like it was calling for something that would never come.

"She had her own bedroom?" Pram said. She didn't know very much about parents, but she knew that they shared bedrooms once they were married.

"It's not a bedroom," Clarence said, turning the knob.

There was a window on the far wall—not a large window but big enough to fill every corner with light. The walls were yellow, but Pram could see parts along the floor and around the radiator that showed they had once been dark green.

There was a daybed in one corner, and bookshelves along two of the walls, and trinkets everywhere. There was a dresser covered in combs and bottles, and pictures laid under a square of glass.

"Which things have moved?" Pram asked.

"Nearly all of them," Clarence said.

Pram's hand hovered over the dresser. She was mindful not to touch anything. She wasn't entirely sure if this would lead her to any ghosts, but she thought it couldn't hurt.

"Was your mother friendly?" Pram asked.

"Very," Clarence said. "She wouldn't mind that you're here in her room. You can say hello, if you want."

"What was her name?"

"Sarah."

"Hello, Sarah," Pram said. "It's okay if you don't want to talk to me. You don't have to. But I'm a pretty good listener."

Pram's hair was like the light, Clarence thought. She nearly disappeared in the brightness of the room. She closed her eyes to listen for his mother, and he was able to stare at her. She had freckles, but they weren't obvious. They could only be seen in the right lighting, and only if he was close enough.

Her lips were light pink, and the room was so silent that he could hear them parting. She was just about to say something when a noise interrupted them.

She opened her eyes. Clarence realized how close they were standing, and his cheeks turned red.

They both heard the front door close and the footsteps coming up the stairs. Clarence's eyes were wide. "Quiet," he whispered. "Come on."

He took Pram by the wrist and hurried her across the room, under the daybed, where they were concealed by a blanket that hung over its edge. The blanket smelled of perfume.

"Why are we hiding?" Pram whispered.

"I'm not allowed in here," Clarence said. "Only the maid comes in, to clean the floor and the windows, and she's careful not to disturb anything."

He heard his father's heavy shoes approaching and hoped he would assume the door had been left open by the maid, who was forgetful sometimes.

But to Clarence's surprise, his father pushed the pale blue door all the way open and then stood there, looking at the way the light reflected from the bottles and mirrors, like bits of dust that had been set on fire.

Then he did something he'd rarely done when Clarence's mother was alive. Something he had forbidden after her death. He entered the room.

The floorboards creaked loudly under his weight. Clarence's mother had been a wisp of a woman, petite and unassuming. The floorboards were startled by her husband's presence.

Clarence's father stood at the dresser for a long time, and then he picked up a glass bottle of perfume and misted the air with it. In a ray of sunlight, the drops were visible as they fell amongst the other things. He held a picture frame next and ran his large, strong hands over the photo inside.

It felt like an eternity before he left, closing the door gently behind him.

Pram was relieved that they hadn't been caught, and she thought Clarence would be as well. But when she looked at him, there were tears in his eyes. And Pram understood, even before he said the words.

"It wasn't a ghost at all."

CHAPTER
9

To find her father, the only tools Pram had were some old photos, a compass (which she wore around her neck for safekeeping), and a name: Maxwell Baines.

And Clarence and Felix, of course.

The air was icy and held the promise of a first snowfall. And shorter days meant that the sky was already darkening by the time they'd made the hour-long walk to the ocean.

The boats were all docked and gently swaying. During the daylight, the boaters could mostly be found in a series of tall buildings that had once been warehouses or factories long ago. But now the only light came from a shanty tavern.

Pram hesitated. Her shoes were just beyond the reach of the tavern's light, and she felt afraid.

But Clarence wasn't going to let Pram back down. He stepped into the light and took her hand.

Felix, who had been three paces behind Pram the whole time, cleared his throat. "Your aunts will wonder where you are," he said.

Pram looked back at him. "You've never cared what they thought before," she said. "You think they're silly."

"All living people are silly," Felix said defensively. "Especially you, worrying so much about someone you've never even met."

Pram spun away from him and joined Clarence in the beam of light. "Felix is being cruel," she told him. "So he's going to wait outside."

"Fine by me," Felix muttered. But it wasn't fine. It very much upset him to watch his only friend in the world holding a living boy's hand. She wasn't the sad and lonely girl he'd known for years. It wasn't that he wanted her to be sad and lonely—only that he'd wanted to be the one to make that sadness go away. But his light tricks and dancing clouds could never do the things a boy with a heartbeat could do. He couldn't even remember what it had been like to have a heart beating in his chest.

Soon Pram would outgrow him entirely. This was only the beginning of things.

Felix watched at the window. If anyone tried to harm her, he could knock a few glasses from the shelves, at least.

Pram squeezed Clarence's hand. Together they pushed open the door to the tavern. A sign above the door read, THE OAK MERMAID. Anything to do with mermaids couldn't be that scary, Pram told herself.

The smell of cigar smoke and fish was the first thing she noticed. Also, the floor was filthy. There was a roar of laughter that rose up like a wave, and it hurt her ears.

"Excuse me," she said. Her voice was immediately lost.

Clarence took a step forward. "Excuse me," he said, much louder, and Pram was impressed. He'd gotten the attention of the men who sat at the bar. They were all broad-shouldered with thick arms.

The man behind the bar tossed a towel over his shoulder and laughed a little. "Have you two lost your way, then?" he said. "The playground's a few miles back." Another roar of laughter.

"We aren't lost, thank you," Pram said politely. "We're looking for a sailor."

"A little young to come here looking for that, love," a waitress said, wielding a tray of drinks on one hand.

Pram didn't understand what this meant, but Clarence had an idea about it.

"His name is Max," Pram said. "Maxwell Baines."

The name was too formal for this lot of sailors; it was regal and they were burlesque. They laughed again, and

Pram began to see them as something other than human. Hyenas that she'd seen in picture books, maybe.

"Go home, sweetheart," the barkeep said. "It must be nearing your bedtime."

Pram couldn't imagine that her father was anything like these men. None of these men would have written such kind letters to a woman they'd left at home.

She sighed, and when she breathed in again, she found that the weight of the entire world sat upon her chest. She turned for the door, and Clarence followed her.

Felix followed a pace behind as they walked home and continued to keep a watchful eye on Pram. He felt awful for how he'd acted, and felt worse to see his only friend so sad.

"What now?" Clarence said.

There was only one more place Pram could think to try when she needed answers. "Maybe next time we can try the library," she said.

The sun had already set, and the lights of the two-hundred-year-old colonial house shone in the distance. As they passed the pond, Felix mumbled his first word since the docks. "Good night," he said.

"Good night," Pram said, not looking back at him. Hand in hand, she and Clarence walked the rest of the way home.

Even before Pram could turn the knob, Aunt Dee and Aunt Nan threw open the door. They were about to scold Pram for being so late, but they had a change of heart when they saw that her hand had just broken away from Clarence's, as though she meant to hide the embrace from them. She also wiped the frown from her face, again a moment too late.

"Come in, come in," Aunt Nan said. "We were starting to worry, and dinner is about to go on the table."

They insisted that Clarence stay for dinner. He tried to decline the offer, as that was the polite thing, but they wouldn't take no for an answer. It was the least they could do. Clarence didn't know the sense of relief he brought to Pram's aunts. He was Pram's first living friend. And he was charming, rich, and very polite to boot. He was just what she needed, they thought. If her mother had met a nice boy like Clarence, things would have turned out differently.

CHAPTER 10

On Saturday afternoon, Pram walked to the library with her father's name in her memory and his compass around her neck.

Clarence and Felix went with her. Felix, who was usually fearful of the world beyond his pond, found that his desire to ensure Pram's safety made him brave; first he'd left his pond to visit the docks, and now the library. This was a big deal for him. He had, after all, been a ghost for a very long time. He no longer remembered what the town had looked like when he was alive. It was like visiting a foreign country.

He was aware of cars because he had seen them driving by his pond. But it was fascinating to see them up close.

A black Cadillac was approaching, and Felix leaped from the sidewalk to touch it. The front of the car looked like a peculiar bug; its lights were eyes that sat on either side of a wide metal smile.

"Felix, no!" Pram yelled. The car hit him, and Pram let out a scream that turned the heads of every pedestrian in the plaza.

The car drove away, and Felix was left standing in the road, his eyes bright with excitement.

"What's the matter?" Clarence asked.

"Never mind," Pram said, her cheeks red with embarrassment and a little bit of anger. "That was a mean trick," she told Felix.

"It wasn't a trick. I only wanted to get a better look," Felix said. He was walking beside her now. "There were children playing in the backseat."

"Don't do it again," Pram said. "I could have had a heart attack."

Clarence patiently walked beside Pram as she had a conversation that didn't include him. He told himself it wasn't fair to be jealous; Felix had a lot of challenges, being a ghost.

A woman bumped into Pram and then hurried on her way, calling apologies. Felix saw the unease on Clarence's face as he asked Pram if she was all right, and it made him feel relieved to know that someone in the living world was looking out for Pram.

Once inside the library, Pram spoke with a librarian, who directed them to the newspaper archives. The newspapers were kept in a back room, and the pages were brittle and dusty.

Pram only knew that her mother's affair with her father must have ended the year Pram was born. She started with the month of her birth and worked backward through the archives. Clarence scanned the same papers a second time, just in case she'd missed anything important. Neither of them knew exactly what they were looking for, but still, it seemed like an injustice when they found nothing.

Felix, who had never learned how to read, sat beside a woman who was reading a story to her children amid the bright covers of children's books. He didn't know what Pram might find in her search, but it worried him. Her aunts would have told her where to find her father if they thought it was a good idea.

It was past noon when Clarence suggested they take a break for lunch. His maid had packed sandwiches. So they sat on the library steps, nibbling at the triangular slices. Felix jumped through puddles in the street, making splashes only Pram could see. Felix was not in the mood to let Clarence and the rest of the living world see his tricks. Pram tried her best not to be sullen.

"Thanks for helping," she said to Clarence. "I know this isn't as exciting as the spiritualists."

After discovering his father had been the one to move his mother's things, and presumably open the bedroom curtains each morning, Clarence had decided to take a reprieve from his search for his mother's ghost. His heart simply could not endure another failure. He was now working his way through the many shades of grief. Sadness made everything gray, he'd learned, but there were different types of gray, some much darker than the others. There were dark spots in his memories he wasn't brave enough to enter.

But Pram was always bright. There was always some sort of light clinging to her. He often thought of her when he was sad.

"It's more informative than the spiritualists," he said. "We're learning some local history."

Pram dropped her chin into her hand. "I guess so."

Felix leaped out of the way of an approaching Volkswagen. He especially liked these because they had the body of a beetle but the snout of a terrier.

As the car blurred past, Felix, with the advantage of being invisible, saw something peculiar. A woman stood on the opposite side of the street, and she was staring at an oblivious Pram. The woman had a long coat that was trimmed with fur, and she was half-hidden by a tree that grew from a box in the sidewalk. Now that Felix was noticing her, he realized that he had seen her on the way to the library, too. She was following them.

He didn't like the way the woman stared. It was his belief that most people were cruel, or at the very least something of which to be suspicious, especially adults. Pram didn't share in this belief, and that worried him. There were few things more dangerous than trust.

He looked back at Pram and Clarence, who were having a conversation and not paying him any mind. Pram might scold him if she knew what he was about to do, so he would have to be subtle.

It wasn't easy for Felix to manipulate objects in a way that the living would notice. When he made the clouds dance for Clarence, all he had done was create an illusion. Ghosts could do this. The living would see something strange for a moment, and then things would be normal again and they'd blame their imaginations. But Felix was determined to be rid of this woman, and so he stood very still, and he concentrated on the tree where the woman stood, until his vision blurred. The leaves began to tremble; the branches quaked. It was a very small tree, and with a final thrust it was uprooted and fell before the woman with a crash.

A baby wailed in its push carriage; a man rushed to the woman in the coat and asked if she was all right. Pram and Clarence snapped to attention. Felix resumed leaping through the puddles.

If Felix had meant to keep the woman away for the moment, he'd succeeded. But if he'd meant to make the woman forget all about Pram, he'd failed. He didn't see the interest on the woman's face as she watched Pram and Clarence on the steps.

CHAPTER 11

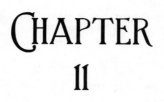

Felix wasn't sure of his limits, if he had limits. After he'd been dead a while, he began to suspect he could swim to the bottom of the oceans. Beyond that. He suspected that he could swim so far down that he'd eventually go through the center of the earth and come out the other side. He could swim into the clouds, into the stars. Maybe there were ghosts on the other planets. Maybe there were ghosts laughing and splashing each other with the heat of the sun. He wasn't brave enough to find out.

It wasn't that he was especially fond of Earth—he wasn't. He had the distinct impression that it hadn't been kind to him when he was alive. But just the same, he'd been human once, and he kept to the restrictions humans had. He'd sat on the kitchen counter and listened to the radio as Pram's aunts made breakfast, though, and the voices in the radio talked of walking on the moon one day. The living were so restless, he thought. The living wanted to get away from their little world, while he wanted to hold on to his.

But if he wanted to hold on to Pram, he would have to leave his limitations. He would follow her. He would be brave. He would stay beside her for as long as she would have him.

He didn't know how long their arrangement could last. One day she would be too old to want him. It was already happening. She was as tall as he was now, and next year she'd be taller. He had watched her for years before she noticed him. As a toddler she would infuriate him by stomping around his tree on her uncertain feet, all as her aunts would stand by and encourage it. She was forever upsetting the quiet to which he'd grown accustomed.

And then, when she was a bit older, she reached for the ghost of a grasshopper that bounced before her. "What have you got?" one of the aunts asked. "There's nothing there." And Pram, frustrated, chased after the thing until it led her to Felix.

She didn't see him, exactly, but as she looked through him, her young eyes showed a curiosity that wasn't ordinary. It took Felix days to work up the courage to touch her hair, and months for her to realize it was not the wind.

It was a delicate balance for the two of them to come to know each other, and months still before she could see him all at once, but she had never been afraid of him. And as he grew to care for this living girl, Felix's exasperation gave way to longing.

He'd made the mistake of caring for a living girl. Time for the living was not the same as it was for the dead. For Pram, growing older was a thing that happened more quickly than she could help. In a blink, her jumper was too short. In another, her hair too long and her shoes too tight. But for Felix, it had been an eternity, marred by the subtle signs that his only friend in the world was getting older.

He thought about this as he followed her home. She was weary from a day of searching through library archives, deflated by unrequited hope. She laid her head on Clarence's shoulder.

Felix knew that he could never like Clarence. Felix might be dead, but he still conformed to some rules of the living, and he could never like a boy he was jealous of. And he was quite jealous, especially of the way that Clarence was there even when he wasn't. Sometimes Pram would be quiet, but there would be a sparkle in her eyes, and Felix would know that she was thinking of her living boy.

When they returned to the house, Pram's aunts once

again insisted that Clarence stay for dinner, to which he politely declined. His father was expecting him at home.

"Tell him we say hello!" Aunt Nan called after him.

Felix followed Pram up the stairs and stood with his arms folded while she scrubbed her face before the mirror. "You almost never come inside," she told him.

"I thought you might need me," he said. "You look sad."

"I'm not," she said, folding the towel neatly and then hanging it from the bar. "Just disappointed."

She stared at her reflection for a long time. She looked like the photo of her mother over the staircase. Felix could see, in that oval of glass, what she would be in ten years. He had seen Pram's mother when she was alive and hadn't thought much of her. She was the youngest daughter living in that old colonial, and she swam in Felix's pond. But she hadn't ever seen Felix, or the ghost insects, and she spent most of her time there below the water's surface. Never spoke a word.

At first, Felix thought the woman who swam in his pond might have been a ghost herself. Though she didn't see him, and though she breathed, he could feel sadness in her that seemed too heavy to belong to anyone in the living world. It surprised him when, years later, the woman's daughter appeared under his tree, shrouded in sunlight.

"Maybe you should wait and find your father when

you're older," Felix said. "Old enough to travel, at the very least."

"I'm nearly twelve," Pram said.

"It doesn't have to be now, is all," Felix said. "You've always been happy here, haven't you?"

"Yes, but I'm not sure I can explain it," Pram said. "All my life I've felt as though I should be something else."

"What else could you possibly be?" Felix said.

Pram looked at him. "A daughter."

Felix had left his heart buried in the ground years and years ago, but he felt it crack apart.

"Don't you see, Felix?" Pram said. "Aunt Dee and Aunt Nan had no choice but to take me in. It wasn't their plan. It just happened. And somewhere out there is the place I was meant to be. I just want to know where that is."

"How do you know you weren't meant to be here?" Felix asked.

"Because my parents aren't here. Isn't that the way it goes? You're born and your parents have a plan for where you should be."

The living were never happy where they were, Felix thought. But he wouldn't know how to explain this to Pram. "What will happen once you find this place?" he asked.

She smiled at that, but the smile quickly faded. "Felix, I worry about you living all alone in that tree. Or not living,

I suppose. Once I've found my father, there won't be anyone to keep you company."

It was one of Felix's greatest fears, but he said, "I'll manage."

"If I'm going to be moving on," Pram said, "maybe it's time for you to think about moving on, too."

"To where?" Felix said.

"You know where," Pram said. "On."

"I wouldn't know how," Felix said. This wasn't entirely true. He had never tried to leave, but he had always felt that the exit would be easy to find if he'd only wanted to find it. The whole truth was that he was afraid.

"I could help you," Pram said. "Clarence will help, too." She ran the tap and flicked a bit of water at him. "Think about it."

Felix did think about it, especially as he sat on the counter, watching Pram and the elders having dinner. It was unusually quiet at the table, Pram being lost in thought as she was.

Aunt Dee and Aunt Nan were quiet, too, and their worried glances at Pram suggested they'd heard her talking to herself when she was in the bathroom. They loved her, Felix knew, or else they wouldn't worry at all, and they would be sad if she left them. But Felix also knew that Pram was right—her aunts had inherited her. Already, at almost twelve, Pram had the bravery to conquer whatever seas stood between her and where she might have been.

Felix could only hope that whatever awaited her would be enough. The idea of Pram's father turning out to be a disinterested nomad sailor was too much to think about. Pram was special; she was the most special thing in the living world, and if her father wasn't able to see that, Felix would want to punch him in the nose.

After dinner, Felix followed Pram to her attic. He blew at the flowers in her wallpaper, and the petals spun around her and settled in her lap. "Thank you," she said.

"If I were to move on, would you ever find another ghost to amuse you as much as I do?" Felix asked.

"No," she said. "Never. But I would think about you all the time. When I was grown up, I would name my first child Felix, even if it was a girl."

"That seems strange, a girl named Felix," Felix said.

"Yes," Pram said. "I've decided strange isn't a bad thing."

She turned out the light and climbed into bed.

CHAPTER 12

Sometimes Felix was a presence in Pram's dreams. She didn't see him, but she felt that he was responsible for the things she did see. She didn't think that he did this on purpose; she dreamed of his thoughts as he wandered around the pond at night. Sometimes they were nice things—women in ruffled crème dresses and manicured poodles on leashes—and sometimes they were not nice things, and Pram would awaken suddenly and the dream would leave her, as though Felix was unconsciously trying to protect her from some awful truth that occurred a century before she was born.

But that night, she had a dream that Felix wasn't responsible for. She dreamed of her mother and a sailor dancing in a circle, on the pedestal of a music box, and a breeze that smelled like burnt autumn air.

Pram thought she was still dreaming when she pulled back the covers, descended the creaky stairs, and went outside. In the haze of sleep, the street lamps were filled with siren songs, each one a bit louder than the last, and she felt certain that something lovely awaited her.

Felix was practicing his bravery by wandering as far as he dared from his tree. He'd made it to the small wooden bridge over the running stream when he saw Pram approaching.

He knew right away that something wasn't right. She was wearing her nightgown and slippers without a coat, and when he ran to her, she didn't say hello. Her eyes were sleepy, a moon reflected in both of them.

"Where are you going so late at night?" he said.

"Shh," she said, and walked around him.

"Can I go with you?"

"Shh."

Worriedly, he followed a pace behind her. She walked in the center of the road, putting one foot squarely ahead of the other, and it was as though she were a marionette, Felix thought. When he tried to steer her away, his hands went through her. They could usually touch each other, but only if they both wanted to at the same time. The dead had no control over the desires of the living, and no way to inhibit them.

Right now, Pram would not allow him. Felix found this especially worrisome.

They walked for what was surely an hour, until they reached the center of town. All the shop windows had the empty quality of Pram's stare, and for the first time in all his years as a ghost, Felix thought he was the one being haunted.

Pram turned down an alleyway, beyond the reach of the street lamps.

"It isn't safe here," Felix said.

She stopped walking, and Felix thought that at last he'd broken through her trance. But then she knocked on a door that was so cleverly hidden by shadows that Felix hadn't realized there was a door there at all. A faded sign read, LADY SAVANT'S SPIRIT SHOW.

A man opened the door. The muscles of his arms were as thick as Felix's tree. The man stepped aside and let Pram enter. He didn't ask for her name and didn't seem unnerved that she was in a trance; he looked up and down the alleyway and closed the door. Felix pushed through it.

They were inside a small room, lit by candles that sat on crates and boxes. In the shadows there were chairs folded and propped against the wall.

Pram, who thought she was dreaming, remembered

this place from the evening she'd spent with Clarence. She could taste chocolate-raspberry ice cream. "I don't have my ticket," she said.

"It's all right, doll," a woman said. The woman was sitting on a cushion on the floor. Felix recognized her as the woman who had been staring at Pram that afternoon.

Pram recognized her as Lady Savant. Without her makeup, Lady Savant was most ordinary, and Pram preferred her this way.

Pram curtsied and said, "Hello."

"Come and sit," the woman said, patting an empty cushion, which had been fashioned from a burlap sack that still smelled like coffee beans. "You may call me Claudette if you prefer the name my mother gave me. What shall I call you?"

"Pram," Pram said.

"What an unusual name." Lady Savant cupped Pram's chin, looked into her vacant eyes. "But then, you're an unusual girl."

Felix paced around them. The woman looked his way, and Felix thought she saw him, but then she looked at Pram again.

"Do you know what you're doing here, Pram?" she asked.

Pram shook her head.

"Ever since the night we met, I've had dreams," Lady

Savant said. "Dreams and visitations from a woman with freckles and white hair like yours. She has asked me to help you."

"Why?" Pram asked.

"She says that she owes you a favor. She says that she's your mother," Lady Savant said.

Pram shook her head again. "My mother's dead," she said. "I think her spirit left because she was angry that I killed her when I was born."

Felix tried to pull Pram's hair to wake her. She sat upright and her eyes were open, but this Lady Savant woman had put her under a spell, for Pram would never tell anyone these things. But his fingers went through her, and her hair remained undisturbed.

"Is that so?" Lady Savant said. "She has been a bit murky on the details. I can't see her very clearly, you understand. But I think you can."

"I've never seen my mother," Pram said. "Only in pictures. My aunts don't like it if I ask about her. They say what's done is done."

"But you see other spirits, don't you?" Lady Savant said.

"Sometimes," Pram said.

"Pram!" Felix said. He stomped and clapped.

"Is there a spirit here now?" Lady Savant asked.

Pram hesitated. Even from deep within her trance, she

knew that Felix was someone she was meant to protect. He was hers.

"It's all right, doll," Lady Savant said. "We've only just met. It's smart of you to be skeptical. I'm the one who invited you; I should be the one doing the explaining."

Felix scowled at the woman, and from the way she arched her shoulders, he could swear she felt it. Good. He wanted her to feel him there. He wanted her to know that Pram belonged to him, and that anyone who messed with her mind was asking for trouble. If he had to haunt the earth for a hundred more years, he would find a way to make her pay for this.

"When I was a young girl like you," Lady Savant said, "I would see spirits everywhere, as plain as if they were standing before me. But then I made a mistake. I told my parents what I was seeing, and they sent me to a special place that stripped me of my ability."

A bit of fear ebbed its way through Pram's trance. She had thought the worst thing that could happen to a girl like her would be the circus. And even the circus didn't seem too terrible. But she had never thought someone could take her ability away. She wouldn't know how to look at the world if she saw only the living.

Felix thought he saw a flash of life in Pram's eyes again. But it was gone quickly.

"My ability has returned a bit over the years," Lady

Savant said. "But it isn't as strong as it was. That's why I can hear only a little of what your mother has to say, and why she's clearest in my dreams."

"What does she say?" Pram asked.

"She says that she's sorry," Lady Savant said. "And that she knows where your father is."

"Where?" Pram asked.

"Far," Lady Savant said. "It would cost a lot of money to get there. More money than a little girl could have. Which is why I've come up with a way to help you. Think of how powerful we would be." She waved her hand across the air as though she were holding the headline on a silver tray: "'Lady Savant and the Child Extraordinaire.' A woman who can hear spirits, and a girl who can see them. We would travel the country, and pay our way with nightly shows."

Pram shrank into herself. She was beginning to awaken, and with consciousness came fear. Whatever hold Lady Savant had over her was waning.

Lady Savant knew it. "You must go home now," she said. "A young girl needs her rest. Tomorrow morning when you awaken, you will remember this dream, and you'll come and see me."

"I'll . . . see you?" Pram said.

"Because you want to find your father," Lady Savant said.

"I want to find my father," Pram echoed. She had no trouble with that part, because it was true.

The man with the muscular arms opened the door. The breeze moved Pram's hair. She stood to leave.

"You'll come back tomorrow," Lady Savant called after her.

Pram walked slowly through the town. Her eyelids were drooping, her feet dragging. Felix wished he were alive so that he could carry her the rest of the way home.

"Pram?" he said, walking circles around her.

She stopped walking and looked at him. "Felix?" she said. And her eyes fluttered and went white, and she collapsed.

CHAPTER 13

Felix was sure he'd entered every Tudor house in the town before he found Clarence, who was sleeping. "You have to wake up," Felix pleaded. "You're the only hope I have." He reached through Clarence's curly head again and again. "You stupid boy."

Normally Felix took comfort in being invisible, but now for the first time he hated it. He hated himself for being dead, and for being helpless. He'd left Pram alone and without a coat, breathing clouds into the chilly air. Deep in her unconsciousness, Pram remembered who Felix was and that she trusted him, and he'd managed to drag her to the sidewalk before her body fell through him again.

In his dream, Clarence saw her there. He dreamed that the howling wind carried a voice telling him that he had to wake up. He knitted his eyebrows together and pulled the blanket tighter around his shoulder.

Felix balled his fists. He thought of hurricanes and willed himself to have the power of one. He'd been able to make the tree fall that afternoon, and he could surely summon a commotion now.

The top drawer of Clarence's dresser slid from its hinge and hit the ground with a thud. Pram disappeared from his dream and he sat up.

"Yes, good," Felix said. "Now go and find her."

But Clarence of course didn't hear him. In the moonlight he saw the drawer on the ground, and he knew that something was amiss. Drawers did not fall on their own. He thought of his dream, which had been unusually vivid, and had the horrible idea that it might be real.

"Hello?" Clarence said. "Felix, is that you?"

Clarence couldn't know that Felix stood beside the bed, shouting and gesturing for the door.

Felix did have to give the boy credit. It was instinct, not a special ability, that made Clarence get out of bed and put on his coat and shoes. There might have been a little bit of love to it, as well, though Felix would never acknowledge as much.

Clarence ran through the house, and just before he reached the front door, a voice called out, "Where are you going?"

One of the maids stood in the doorway of her bedroom, her hair disheveled.

"To the center of town," Clarence said. "It's an emergency."

"What kind of emergency could require a boy to be out alone this late at night?"

"I don't have time to explain," Clarence said, opening the door.

"If you leave, I'll have to tell your father," the maid said.

"Yes, thank you," Clarence said. "He wouldn't believe it coming from me."

With that, he was out the door. He was an excellent runner; before his mother died, he'd run nearly every day, and now even without the practice, he was fast as ever. He felt a wind at his back that wasn't entirely normal, and he knew that Felix was steering him in the right direction.

"Where is she?" Clarence asked. And then, as though Felix could answer, he saw Pram in her nightgown, lying just outside a street lamp's glow.

"Pram!"

He knelt at her side, gasping and flushed.

She was in a deep sleep and shivering from the cold. He tried to wake her, but her shoulders fell heavily against his arm when he lifted her, and her head rolled back.

She was exactly as she had been in his dream, and now

Clarence felt that he must have been dreaming still. He had never seen Pram look so gray, as though she were a machine that had been turned off. It was with disbelief that he took off his coat and wrapped it around Pram's shoulders.

He touched her cold cheek. "What's happened to you?" he said.

The headlights of a car shone in Clarence's eyes.

The doorbell rang several times, followed by a knock that held all the authority one would expect from a man of Mr. Blue's status. It was the authority of that knock that got Aunt Dee and Aunt Nan from their beds. They hurried down the stairs, complaining and fussing about the commotion.

The aunts opened the door and gasped. They had been certain Pram was safe in her bed, and yet there she was, sleeping in a strange man's arms. They might have screamed for the police, except that Clarence Blue was there, and from the man's curly hair it was obvious the strange man must be his father.

"I'm sorry," Mr. Blue said. "When I drove by, she was sleeping on the sidewalk. I'm not sure what happened. Clarence insists she's a friend of his, and that she belongs to you."

As Aunt Nan retrieved Pram from Mr. Blue's arms, Pram opened her eyes just long enough to get a look at Mr. Blue and whisper, "Are you my father?"

If Mr. Blue had a response to this, it was buried in the nervous laughter of the aunts. "The poor thing is a sleepwalker," Aunt Dee said.

"Been happening for as long as she could walk," Aunt Nan said, furthering the lie. After eleven years of caring for Pram, they'd developed a sense of creativity so they could conceal her eccentricities.

"We used to find her in the pantry some mornings, hugging the flour like it was a little teddy bear," Aunt Dee said. "And always muttering nonsense."

"Thank you again, and so sorry for the trouble." Aunt Nan closed the door on Mr. Blue's startled expression and Clarence's worried eyes.

The aunts stared at Pram, still wearing Clarence's coat, and then they stared at each other.

Pram had always been a peculiar child. She had imaginary friends, and she wasn't frightened of the things little girls ought to be frightened of. But nothing like this had ever happened. The aunts had believed that with enough patience and their best efforts, they could keep Pram safe from a world that would be cruel to her. The world had been crueler to Pram's mother than Pram would ever know.

But now they weren't so sure they could protect her.

They carried her to bed and tucked the blankets to her chin. They made certain the windows were locked and the door downstairs was latched. Aunt Nan took a bear from the shelf and placed it on Pram's bed.

She looked like a normal girl for the moment, Aunt Nan thought. A normal girl who was safe and asleep and dreaming of ribbons.

She looked like her mother, Aunt Dee thought.

Aunt Dee and Aunt Nan didn't speak of their younger sister, or the cruel manner of her death, and especially not the part where she nearly took Pram with her. They didn't speak of the sailor who'd told her nice things and then left. Or the sadness in her eyes and in her heart, or how for the last months of her life she didn't speak a word.

But while Pram and her mother had both been strange, Pram had never seemed sad. She was gentle and kind and bright, and so the aunts had hope that she would turn into a lovely sort of woman one day. But that night's actions had the aunts thoroughly afraid. They pinched her cheeks and left her to sleep, and they spent the night whispering at the kitchen table and compiling a list of rules:

No more school—it was clearly too overwhelming.
No more adult books—they gave her too many ideas.

No more imaginary friends—she had a fine friend in the Blue boy now.

No more pond—this was where Pram spent most of her time talking to herself.

And most importantly: *No more talk of ghosts.*

CHAPTER 14

Pram awoke with sunlight in her eyes and a feeling like she needed to be someplace important.

The flowers in the wallpaper were rustling on a breeze. "Felix?" she said.

One of the flowers spiraled away from the wall and landed on her shoulder. By the time she reached for it, it was gone. How strange, she thought. Felix was the only one who did such things, and she could swear she felt him nearby, but she couldn't see him. She crawled under the bed to be certain he wasn't playing a hiding game. "Felix?" She opened her window and called out into the cool morning air, "Felix? I don't like this game."

The door opened, but it wasn't Felix. "Close the window," Aunt Nan said. "You'll catch cold."

Pram did as she was told, and her worried frown was reflected in the glass.

"Who were you talking to just now?" Aunt Nan asked.

"No one," she said, distressed to know this was the truth. She watched the tree from her window but saw no trace of her best friend.

"I thought we might have a talk, then, you and me," Aunt Nan said, sitting on Pram's bed.

Pram pulled the chair away from her desk and sat. "Am I in trouble?" she asked. She couldn't think why she would be but felt inexplicably that she was.

"No," Aunt Nan said. "But I think we should talk about last night." She looked at Pram and could see in her eyes that she didn't understand. "Do you remember last night?"

Pram didn't remember, though she could taste the crisp night air on her tongue. She wasn't sure how to answer, so she didn't.

"Do you remember having unusual dreams?" Aunt Nan said.

Pram always had unusual dreams, so she said, "Not especially." She moved her shoulders uncomfortably. Many things weren't right about this morning; she wasn't used to being questioned, and her feet ached, and she wanted to look for Felix.

"There won't be any school from now on," Aunt Nan said, forcing a smile. "That ought to cheer you up, right?"

"No school? Why?"

"Your aunt Dee and I are worried that it's too much for you," Aunt Nan said. "We'll be speaking with Ms. Appleworth and letting her know that you'll resume home schooling."

"It isn't too much for me." Pram was thinking of Clarence. "Honestly."

"It's just that we're concerned for you," Aunt Nan said.

"Don't scare the girl," Aunt Dee said. She was standing in the doorway with a tray of oatmeal and toast. The aunts had also decided that Pram should no longer have desserts for breakfast and lunch, no matter how guilty they might have felt. "There's nothing to be concerned about at all. Only growing pains."

"Growing pains?" Pram asked.

"I had imaginary friends when I was about your age," Aunt Dee said, setting the tray in Pram's lap. "It was difficult for me to let them go. But I was much better for it."

"I don't have any imaginary friends," Pram said, feeling wounded.

"Felix, wasn't it?" Aunt Nan said.

Pram had told her aunts about Felix when she was five years old, too young to realize that certain things should remain a secret. She hadn't mentioned him in years, but sometimes, when she and Felix were talking, she would hear a floorboard creak and suspect someone had been eavesdropping.

"Oh," she said. "Felix hasn't been around for a while."

"Just as well," Aunt Nan said. "He was fine when you were little, but you've outgrown him now."

"You should spend more time with the Blue boy," Aunt Dee said. "He must have other friends he could introduce you to."

He didn't, not anymore, but Pram could see that this was important to her aunts, and she didn't want them to worry. "Okay," she said, feeling scrutinized. Pram couldn't know her aunts' worry; she had spent her entire life worrying that she could never be the woman her mother had been, while her aunts had worried that she would. And now that she was getting taller, and her face more angled, they worried more than ever. And so they did something for Pram that they had never done for their younger sister. They stood and each kissed one of her cheeks, and they said together, "We love you," for the first and perhaps only time.

The cold taste on Pram's tongue spread down her throat and into her lungs, and despite her thick sweater, the chill wouldn't leave her. Her nose was running, and she didn't understand why. She also didn't understand why her aunts wouldn't allow her to go outside, or why they'd laid the subtle hint that she should no longer speak to Felix.

When there came a knock at the door, sometime after three o'clock, Pram somehow knew that it would be for her. She raced past her aunts to open the door.

Clarence stood on the front step with his hands in his pockets. His cheeks were flushed, and Pram could tell he'd been running.

She sniffled. "Hello," she said.

"Hello," Clarence said. "You weren't in school, so I came to check on you."

"Isn't that nice?" Aunt Dee said. "Pram, don't stand there gaping. Let the boy in."

Pram blushed and stepped aside for him. "We'll be upstairs," she said. She took Clarence's hand without giving it a thought, and as she led him up the stairs, she didn't look back to see the way her aunts smiled at the pair of them. And she didn't see that the photo of her mother had gone crooked, as though it was trying to tell her something.

Pram led Clarence into her closet. She turned on the light and closed the door.

"Something bad has happened to Felix," she said.

"What could have happened?" Clarence said. He didn't know much about ghosts, but he presumed that they couldn't be kidnapped or killed.

"I don't know, but he's gone," Pram said. "And my aunts are acting strange. They won't let me out of the house, and they told me that I had outgrown Felix." She dabbed her runny nose with her sleeve. "And all day I've had a chill, and I don't know why."

"You really don't remember?" Clarence said. "About last night?"

"What's to remember?" Pram said.

"You were sleepwalking," Clarence said. "That's how your aunts explained it when my father and I brought you home."

Pram went pale with worry. "I dreamed I went to see Lady Savant," she said. "She said she had been speaking with my mother and that I should visit her again."

"It must not have been a dream," Clarence said. "You must have really been to see her."

Pram chewed on her bottom lip.

"What could it mean?" Clarence asked.

"I don't know. But there has to be a reason she wants to see me. Maybe it has to do with Felix."

Clarence thought about Pram lying unconscious on the sidewalk late at night, and it made him uneasy to think Lady Savant could have had something to do with it. Pram was an extraordinary girl—one who thought nothing of speaking to ghosts—and it would be dangerous for the wrong sort of people to know about her. "I don't like it," he said.

"Something strange is happening," Pram said. "I've never sleepwalked, and Felix has never hidden from me like this. I have to see Lady Savant and find out what she wants from me."

"Didn't she tell you?" Clarence asked.

"I can't remember. I thought I was dreaming. When I woke up, what she'd said sort of . . . flew away."

Clarence frowned. "If you see her, I'm coming with you. I'm the one who took you to her show in the first place."

Pram squeezed his hands. "Thank you," she said. "It will have to be after my aunts have gone to bed. They won't let me outside right now, even if it's with you."

"What time, then?" Clarence asked. It would be easy for him to leave in the middle of the night, assuming he didn't wake the maids.

"Ten thirty," Pram said. "By the pond."

CHAPTER 15

Clarence arrived at the pond at ten thirty exactly. It was especially cold, and the remaining leaves of Felix's tree seemed to be in a state of panic. "Hello, if you can hear me," Clarence said to Felix. "Pram is very worried, you know."

He heard footsteps, and he hoped it would be Felix, whom he had never seen. It was strange that he didn't even know what Felix looked like. But Pram was the one to step out of the shadows.

"Sorry I'm late," she said. "I had to be sure Aunt Nan was snoring." She looked up at the leaves and frowned.

"Is he here?" Clarence asked.

"I don't know," she said. "The other day I had talked to him about moving on, and now I'm afraid he's gone because of me."

"He wouldn't leave without saying good-bye," Clarence said.

"No," Pram said. But she couldn't help feeling that she was to blame.

They walked toward the center of town. Pram kicked pebbles and said very little.

Above them, the stars shifted in their sky. Neither of them looked up to notice.

"Pram?" Clarence said. "When did you start seeing them? Ghosts, that is."

"When I was a baby, I think," she said. "It's hard to know. It's like if I asked you when you realized you were human."

Clarence considered this.

"It's just a part of me," she said.

"A gift, then," Clarence said.

Pram shrugged. "Sometimes it's nice," she said. "Sometimes it makes me sad." She didn't know about the dogwood tree in front of the hospital, nor did she know that she was brought into the living world as silent and as gray as the ashes in the fireplace. All Pram knew was that she was tethered to the murky place between this world and the one that comes after it. How this came to be wasn't important to her.

"It sounds like a burden," Clarence said. "But I think it's amazing."

For the first time all night, a smile shone through Pram's worried expression. "You're the only one who hasn't thought it was strange. It bothers my aunts, so I try to pretend like I'm normal, but they know anyway."

"They just mean to protect you," Clarence said.

"Yes," Pram said. "But I think it makes them sad that I can't be like other children."

They'd reached the alleyway that led to Lady Savant's Spirit Show. Pram took a deep breath and held it.

Clarence took her hand.

"You don't have to go in," he said.

"Yes, I do," Pram said, and stepped forward.

She raised her fist to knock on the door, but it opened before she could. The man with thick arms looked at Clarence. "The invitation is only for the girl."

"I'm not letting her go in alone," Clarence said. It was brave of him, Pram thought. The man at the door unnerved her.

"It's okay, Brutus. The boy can come in." Lady Savant sat on a coffee sack, waiting for them. She was not wearing her theatrical makeup, and when Pram saw her face, she remembered from her not-dream that her real name was Claudette. "Come in. Have a seat."

Pram and Clarence shared a coffee sack and were so close to each other that their shoulders touched.

"You're the boy who came to one of my shows with Pram," she said.

Pram vaguely recalled telling Lady Savant her name. It made her uneasy and a little mad to know she'd been tricked into thinking she was dreaming.

"Yes," Clarence said.

"You were looking for your mother, I believe," Lady Savant said. "Did you ever find her?"

"No," Clarence said, pretending it didn't hurt to talk about it. "I fear she's moved on."

"Most of us do," Lady Savant said. "Those who stay usually have something important to attend to. So important that they're able to ignore that force imploring them to move on. Very few will stay just for the sake of staying, though some are too scared to move on right away, and animals seem to enjoy haunting this world. When I was a girl, there was a tomcat's ghost that ran around the apartment building, spooking the mice. He was my first." She looked at Pram. "You remember your first ghost, too, don't you?"

"Insects," Pram said.

"But your first real ghost," Lady Savant said.

"Yes, I remember," is all Pram said.

"There's no need to be secretive," Lady Savant said. "I've been acquainted with your friend Felix."

"You have?" Pram said.

"We had a chat last night. He'd wanted my help moving on."

Pram was certain her heart stopped beating in her chest. "Moving on?"

"He felt that it was time, and he needed me to show him the way. There's nothing to worry about; I've done it dozens of times. You'll learn to guide spirits, too. I can teach you."

Pram couldn't speak, so Clarence was the one to ask, "Can Felix come back? If he changes his mind? Or for visits?"

Lady Savant laughed. "If spirits could come back anytime they pleased, the planet might sink through the stars with the weight of them. No, he's quite gone."

Pram's bones were aching. Her eyes were sore, but she was too stunned to fill them with tears. "He didn't say good-bye."

"It's more common than you think," Lady Savant said. "He told me that you'd always been so kind to him and that he'd been wanting to leave for some time, but it was your face that made him want to stay."

It didn't sound like Felix. "I thought he was afraid of leaving," Pram said.

"Afraid of leaving you," Lady Savant said. "But it was

time. He knows that you're growing too old for him now. He wants you to go on living. He was glad that you would be coming to see me, so that I could help you find your father."

Pram was born orphaned, but she'd been fortunate, at least, that her losses came when she was too young to remember them. She had never lost someone who was a part of her every day, and the grief came too suddenly for her to realize that it was grief. *Felix will be at his tree*, she thought. *I'll go home and find him there.*

Clarence said, "How will you help Pram find her father?"

"You wanted us to raise money doing spirit shows," Pram remembered from her not-dream. "And we'd travel."

"Travel, yes," Lady Savant said. "But our journey would be guided by your mother's spirit."

"I thought Pram's mother had moved on," Clarence said.

"She was away," Lady Savant said. She looked at Pram. "Your mother was troubled when she was alive. She made mistakes, and she has regrets, and it was too painful for her to watch you growing up."

"Why has she come back now, then?" Pram asked.

"Because she was at my show the night you attended. She frequents them. Though she had never seen you before, she knew right away that you were her daughter. She feels that she owes it to you to help you find your father."

Her father had been all Pram could think about for some time, but now the hope of finding him paled in comparison to losing Felix. How could he leave without saying good-bye? Had he tried to tell her he was ready to move on, and she'd missed the signs?

Something about this didn't seem right, and Pram wanted to go home. She wasn't certain she wanted to come back.

"I can't leave without writing a note for my aunts," Pram said. "So they won't worry so much." She stood, and Clarence stood with her. "And I'd need to pack. I should plan this before I make a decision."

"What's to decide?" Lady Savant said, though something about her tone made Pram think it wasn't a question. She thought of what Felix had said about her being sent off to the circus if she told anyone about her abilities. She thought about her strange dream that wasn't a dream at all, and she felt that Lady Savant had cheated her out of her secrets. And Pram didn't know very much about Lady Savant, but she knew enough not to trust her. She didn't trust anyone who took money to speak to ghosts, and she didn't quite believe what she'd said about Felix wanting to move on, even though Felix was nowhere to be found. Pram wondered if Lady Savant had done something to him.

"I've changed my mind," Pram said. "I don't want to find my father. I want to go back."

The man with the thick arms had closed the door. His face was in the shadows, but Pram could see his lips were set in an immovable line. Slowly those lips became a smile.

"Oh," Lady Savant said, "but there is no going back now."

CHAPTER
16

Lily,

*I see your exquisite face at every port. I've made a
horrible mistake leaving you behind. Forgive me,
forgive me, forgive me.*

Max

Pram had memorized her father's words to her mother,
and she recited them over and over in her head, until the
words began to feel distant, and Max and Lily became silhouettes being swallowed by sunlight. They were strangers to her, for they had been in love before she was born,
and before she ever could have mattered to them.

Perhaps she'd made a mistake pursuing her father. Perhaps he was angry with her. She had been more intrusion than daughter to him—the thing that went wrong.

Her breath was shuddering. She drew her knees to her chest.

It was dark, and Clarence couldn't see her tears, but he sensed them and he said, "Don't cry. It'll be all right."

She sniffed. "I've been stupid," she said.

"No more stupid than me looking for my mother's ghost," Clarence said.

He was in the crate next to hers and they were covered by thick blankets, in a caravan filled with folding chairs and boxes from Lady Savant's show.

Pram held her fingers before her face but could see nothing. She thought of Felix moving on, and she hoped there was something other than darkness waiting for him.

"Do you think it's true what Lady Savant said about Felix moving on?" she asked.

"You know him better than I do," Clarence said, "but it doesn't sound right to me. Felix loves you. He wouldn't leave without a proper good-bye. Could Lady Savant have forced him?"

Pram frowned. "I don't think anyone has that power. I think it has to be a choice. But I don't know; I've never helped anyone move on before."

"We'll find out soon," Clarence said as the caravan moved forward through the night.

"I think we'll find out a lot of things," Pram said.

They hadn't fought when Lady Savant and the man with thick arms guided them into the crates. Their silence might have been taken for fear, and while it was true that Pram and Clarence were afraid, the bigger truth was that they were curious. They knew Lady Savant was devious, but they also understood that she could show them a great many things about what comes after life. And both Pram and Clarence had someone dead they wanted to speak to.

Pram wiped at her eyes. "I'm sorry for taking your seat that day," she said. "And for getting you into this mess."

She could hear Clarence shifting in his crate. "I'll never be sorry for that," he said. "I'm glad we're friends."

Pram rested her head against the wall of the crate and pretended it was his shoulder. "I'm glad for that, too."

After a pause, Clarence said, "Felix was trying to protect you. That's why he didn't seem to like me very much."

"He only gets jealous," Pram said.

"It was more than that," Clarence said. "He knew how special you are. He thought the wrong sort of person would come along and cause trouble for you, if they knew about your ability to see ghosts. And he was right. I'm the one who led you to Lady Savant."

"This isn't your fault," Pram said.

But she worried that at least some of what Clarence had said was true. Felix had been trying to protect her, and in terms of both the living and the spirit world, he was the only one who could. But now, suddenly, he was nowhere to be found.

Pram slept and dreamed that she was adrift upon a dark sea. There were no stars, but she knew that she was moving away from home. There was something as heavy as a stone around her neck.

She awoke clutching her father's compass.

The caravan jolted and creaked as it hit a dip in the road.

"Clarence?" Pram said. When he didn't immediately reply, she thought he had been swallowed by the darkness like Felix had been, and she began to panic. "Clarence!"

Something rustled. "I'm here," Clarence replied sleepily. And then, "I think we've stopped moving."

Had they? Pram couldn't tell. She still felt like she was drifting in the waters she had dreamed.

There was the sound of metal doors opening on their hinges, and Pram could see a bit of light stealing in around the blanket's edges.

Someone threw back the blanket. All the whiteness blinded Pram, and after a moment Lady Savant began to appear, her hair wild like the shadow of an angry flame.

Pram could smell the chilly morning air. Her aunts were up before the sun, and they'd surely discovered she was missing by now. They would be looking for her, but they might not go to the police right away, Pram thought. They would think she'd done something silly, and they would hope to find her without attracting too much attention, so that another Ms. Appleworth wouldn't come to take her away.

Pram wondered how long it would take her aunts to realize that something was really wrong. But even that realization wouldn't help them find her. She didn't know where she was herself. She stiffened her shoulders and did her best to look brave.

"Good morning, doll," Lady Savant said. "So dreadfully sorry for the squalid accommodations. We were driving through a city famous for its thieves, and they love children. Do unspeakable things to them. It was much safer for you to blend in among the collection of a silly spirit show's props."

The man with the thick arms climbed into the caravan. It shuddered under his weight, and the vibrations were in tandem with Pram's pounding heart. But she felt a little better when the blanket was lifted over Clarence's crate and a strip of sunlight illuminated his blue eyes. Something about his eyes always calmed her.

She reached through the slats in her crate, and he did the same, and their hands touched for a moment before the man with the thick arms lifted Clarence's crate and carried him away. Pram crawled after him, as though she could follow. "Where are you taking him?"

"Not to worry," Lady Savant said. She was wielding a crowbar, and Pram flinched, but Lady Savant used it only to pry away the lid of Pram's prison.

Even after the lid was gone, Pram hesitated.

Lady Savant laughed. "Come out, silly girl," she said. "You can ride up front with me now. If anyone asks, we'll say you're my niece; won't that be fun?"

The idea only made Pram lonely for her real aunts. Now that she was so far from that two-hundred-year-old colonial, she realized it was the only place in which she'd ever felt safe. That house and the pond where she'd met Felix.

"If I come out, will you tell me more about where Felix has gone?" Pram asked.

"There isn't much to tell," Lady Savant said. "He's moved on. But I can tell you more about the spirit world if you wish."

It would have to do.

Pram climbed from the crate on unsteady legs. Lady

Savant took her hand. Her fingers were plump and soft, and she smelled like every perfume that would ever fit atop a woman's vanity. Her hair and face were done up, but none of this could conceal the menacing edge in her stare. Pram had seen that edge for the first time the night before, and it couldn't be unseen.

As Pram hopped from the back of the caravan, she was greeted with a sky that was robin's-egg blue and the sound of wind weaving through barren branches. Tire tracks sliced parallel lines through a dirt path that was hardly a proper road, and there was no evidence of a city nearby. There was only a lake, the sky's reflection rippling on its surface.

Felix? Pram called to him. She had never tried to summon him with her thoughts, but it was worth trying. He usually seemed to know when she wanted him around. The wind shifted, and the branches bowed away from her. No ghosts. Only air.

The man with the thick arms held Clarence's crate as though it weighed nothing. Clarence gripped the slats, and Pram could see anxiousness on his face. She took a step toward him, but Lady Savant gripped her by the elbows. "It's best if you look away," Lady Savant said.

"What are you going to do with him?" Pram said, though her sweaty palms and chilled blood already knew the answer.

"There's no room for him," Lady Savant said. "He has nothing to offer, and I've no interest in toting an ordinary boy with me."

"Then let him go." Pram's voice was shrill. "Just leave him here. He doesn't have to come with us."

"Pram," Clarence called to her. "Pram, run!"

But she couldn't. There was no escaping that caravan.

"He knows quite a bit, doesn't he?" Lady Savant said. "He knows about your gift, and he knows all about us."

"He won't tell." Pram looked at Clarence, who she could see was trembling. The crate shook in its captor's arms. "He's known about me for months, and he's never breathed a word."

"I need to know for certain that he won't," Lady Savant said, and nodded at the lake. With a swing of brute force, the man threw the crate into the water.

"No!" Pram tried to run for the water, but Lady Savant's grip was cruelly immovable.

Pram struggled and screamed, but there weren't even birds left in the trees to hear her. And for one awful moment, her body went still enough to watch the last corner of the crate disappear below the water's edge. An eruption of bubbles replaced it.

Her screams turned into hiccuping sobs, but in her head her voice was still screaming, *Felix! Felix, please! Where are you?*

Lady Savant had to drag Pram, who was thrashing her legs, into the front of the caravan. The man with the thick arms sat at the wheel. Droplets of lake water freckled his face like gravedigger's dirt.

Pram knelt in her seat and watched the lake through the window as they drove away. They turned a corner and the lake was gone.

She held her breath, trying to calculate how long it would take for Clarence to drown. She hoped that it would be painless and quick, but before long, her temples throbbed and her chest was burning.

She gasped air back into her lungs and hated herself for it.

Lady Savant played with Pram's hair as they rode on. "Shall I tell you about the spirit world now?"

Pram was too heartsick to speak. She'd tucked her father's compass under her shirt, and her skin had warmed it so that it felt like a hard, still heart that had fallen out of her. She was a clock that had been disassembled. Even the dead couldn't put her back together again.

Felix . . . Her mind had been calling him for miles.

A few times, feeling exceptionally desperate, she'd even tried calling her mother. *Lily? Lily, it's me. Your daughter. Did you know you had a girl before you died?* But of course her mother didn't answer. Had she been the one to tell Lady Savant to throw Clarence into the lake out of revenge, because Pram had taken her away from the living world?

"For a living person to enter the spirit world would be like falling into a deep, deep sleep," Lady Savant went on.

Pram wondered if Clarence's ghost would come to her. She worried he wouldn't be able to find her, speeding down that non-road, miles from anywhere they knew.

"As a living person who can see spirits, you can develop the strength to peer into the spirit world. You enter a trance and leave your body behind."

Pram didn't want to listen to anything Lady Savant said; she despised this woman who had destroyed the only friends she had in the world. But she could see what was being described, as though she was being given directions down a road she'd forgotten she once traveled. She felt herself drifting away from the words, and away from the car, until she could no longer feel the weight of her bones.

She could see the souls drifting on either side of her, curled up, asleep. Each one of them was a world of its own design. In their sleep the souls twitched or smiled or cried without sound.

Pram forgot the traveling caravan. She forgot Lady Savant's voice. She drifted into the spirit world without feet to carry her, or hands to touch, or skin to hold her together. But she could find no one she recognized. The faces were blurry, and some of the bodies were turned away from her. She saw notches in spines, and jutting shoulder blades, and she tasted smoke and water and fear.

Felix? she called. *Lily?*

Clarence? To call his name left an aching in her bodiless soul. He did not belong here. Not for years and years.

No one heard her, and all the spirits were strangers.

Pram felt herself flying backward. She fell into her body again with a force that rattled her bones. The caravan had stopped, and through smeared vision Pram could see Lady Savant sitting over her, feeling her neck for a pulse.

"Did we kill her?" the man with the thick arms said. His voice was far away. He sounded afraid, which was odd, Pram thought. He had no trouble killing Clarence. Why should her life matter?

"Of course not," Lady Savant said. "She's a strong thing. I could tell the moment I saw her. She has a defiant chin."

"She doesn't look too good."

"Just drive."

Pram stared at the caravan's ceiling. The leaves and sunlight put on a shadow show for her.

"What did you see?" Lady Savant asked.

Pram wouldn't tell her. She would never tell her anything again.

The sky turned cloudy; fat drops of rain hit the roof of the caravan, each one like a body falling down. Pram watched lightning draw a hard line into the horizon.

For the dozenth time, Lady Savant touched Pram's forehead and tsked. "Perhaps I've pushed you too far too soon."

Pram wondered how her aunts were getting on, and if they'd phoned the police by now.

She thought of Clarence's father, and the sadness she could feel in him when he rearranged his wife's things that day she and Clarence hid under the daybed.

Lady Savant prattled on about what a prodigy Pram was, and how prosperous they'd be, and how strong she would be when she was older, and Pram began to realize that Lady Savant was not going to help her find her father. That had only been a lie to lure her away from home. She would kill an innocent boy just to keep a girl who could talk to ghosts, as though she were a pet.

Pram closed her eyes. She tried to return to the spirit world just to have a moment's reprieve from this horrid caravan.

Instead, she entered a dream that was not a dream. She was skating across a frozen pond, and she brought her hands to her face to smell the cold wool of her mittens. Her hair was long and red and braided. A woman called to her from somewhere beyond the pond's edge. She tried to hear the name, but before she could, everything turned black and dreamless.

CHAPTER 17

When she awoke, Pram saw ribbons of black cast iron over her head and around her like bony fingers. The ground tilted under her when she moved.

She gasped and crawled backward until her back was pressed against the bars. She was in a cage, not unlike the one that had housed Frances, a canary that had belonged to one of the elders years ago.

Her shallow, panicked breaths echoed in the blackness. Above her, the chain creaked and groaned.

The cage was lined with a soft mattress made of silk. It smelled heavily of lavender.

Am I in the spirit world? she asked, to no one in particular. She was too frightened to speak aloud.

A flame lantern had been left in the cage, and by

looking at the pool of melted wax, Pram knew she had been asleep for a long time.

She hugged her knees to her chest. Her heart was beating double in her ears, and as she'd always done, Pram tried to tell herself that the extra heart belonged to her mother. But she realized now how silly that idea had been. She was alone. More alone than she ever thought possible.

"Hello?" a voice said.

Two hands grabbed the bars of Pram's cage. She flinched and gripped at her skirt. "Don't be afraid." Between the two hands, a young man's face came closer to the bars and brought itself into the light. He couldn't have been older than sixteen.

Pram swallowed hard. "Did you need me to help you with something?" she asked.

"Why do you think I need your help?"

"Because you're dead," Pram said. Slowly, she uncurled her limbs and sat up straighter.

"Oh, that," the young man said. "Sorry if it frightens you."

"It makes me feel better, actually," Pram said. With ghosts she at least knew what to expect. The living were the ones still capable of harm. "What's your name?"

"I can't remember," he said.

"What would you like to be called, then?" Pram asked.

"Finley," the young man said. "That's what everyone around here calls me."

Everyone? Pram wondered but didn't ask. She fanned out her skirt pleats into a curtsy. "I'm Pram."

Finley smiled, and Pram felt herself smiling back. There was something about him that calmed her, even though his left temple was blackened and bloody; a faint smell of smoke told Pram that he'd died in a fire. She couldn't always tell how a ghost had died; sometimes they didn't remember their deaths, and they appeared as they last remembered themselves to be, like Felix. Animals also came out unscathed. Pram once witnessed a badger get hit by a car. As its body lay damaged and red on the ground, its spirit arose and scurried off into the woods, wholly intact, as though a minor thing such as death couldn't interrupt its plans.

"Is there a reason you came to me?" Pram asked.

"You asked a question," Finley said. "I didn't hear all of it. I've been busy with this falling star. I've been expecting it to drop for days now, and I wanted to be nearby when it finally came down. If I listen hard enough, I can hear the wishes people make. It's nice to hear the living all at once."

It sounded wonderful, and also sad, Pram thought. "I asked if I was in the spirit world."

"You look alive to me," Finley said. "Anyway, I don't need help. You're the one who looks like she needs help."

Pram willed herself not to cry. "A woman who calls herself Lady Savant brought me here. She told me she was going to help me find my father, but now I see she just wanted to lure me away from home."

"Oh, her," Finley said. "She does like to take things that don't belong to her."

"What does she want from me?" Pram said.

Footsteps echoed on a hard floor. "You're sure to find out," Finley said. "Those are her heels clacking on the marble."

Pram paled with fear.

Finley slipped between the bars of Pram's cage and sat beside her. "Don't be afraid," he said. "You seem like such a brave girl, talking to a ghost."

"She killed my friend," Pram said. Saying the words aloud meant accepting what had happened. Her arms shook as she hugged her knees again. "She stood back and did nothing as he drowned."

"Could your friend see ghosts?" Finley asked. "Or read palms? Anything?"

"No," Pram said. "He didn't have any abilities, and he wasn't going to hurt anyone."

"She won't drown you," Finley said. "Not if you have something she wants. She only kills useless things."

"Clarence wasn't useless," Pram said. "I loved him."

Saying it aloud was an admission as well. No wonder she'd grown up in a house where nobody said they loved anyone; what a terrible pain that word caused.

Finley patted her shoulder. "I'm sure he was a fine friend."

Pram could hear a skeleton key rattling in a lock. It blocked a small bit of light that had been shining through the keyhole.

Finley disappeared. Pram looked over both shoulders for him, but he was gone.

The chain holding the cage creaked, and Pram tried to keep still if only to make it stop. She was sure she'd heard something like it in her nightmares.

The door swung open, creating a triangle of light from the hallway that spread out to reveal green wallpaper with silver insects that gleamed and appeared to be almost crawling.

"Awake now, are you?" Lady Savant said. "Good, good. I knew you'd be fresh as a daisy after a little rest."

Pram saw something move beside the door, where the light thinned and turned the insects black. Two long dark braids swung across the darkness, trailing a girl who chased after a firefly that had come out of the wall. She giggled and disappeared into the shadows.

Lady Savant didn't notice her. "There's no electricity,

but once the sun comes up, you'll see that this room is very pretty," she said. "Would you like to come out and have a better look?"

Pram didn't answer. Any word she'd ever spoken to that woman had caused her trouble. She would rather talk to the ghosts in the shadows—Finley with his burns, and the little girl chasing insects.

And yet, despite knowing better, there was something within Pram that wanted to like Lady Savant. Her fragrance was intoxicating and sweet. Her eyes were as kind sometimes as they were cruel other times.

"Come on, now," Lady Savant said. "There's no reason to be frightened. There's a staircase just outside your little door, see?"

Despite her bitterness, Pram couldn't help peering beyond the arched door of her prison. An iron staircase, inlaid with flower shapes, reached down toward the darkness of the floor. She was curious about where the stairs led. Curious, and suddenly very hungry.

"Come out," a giggling voice said. The girl with the black hair leaned sideways into the light of the doorway. She waved shyly and scurried off again.

Well, Pram thought, she wouldn't mind having something to eat.

But she wasn't going to speak.

CHAPTER
18

Pram walked barefoot down a hallway with a cold tile
floor. Flames on sconces illuminated ovals of wallpaper
on either side of her. She felt as though she were dreaming,
and in this dream she wore a green plaid dress and yellow
ribbons that streamed from her ponytail to down in front
of her shoulders.

She heard the footsteps of the girl with dark hair
behind her. The girl was skipping and singing:

Hush-a-bye, don't you cry
Go to sleepy, little baby
When you wake, you shall have
All the pretty little horses

Way down yonder in the meadow
Lies a poor little lambie
Bees and butterflies, picking out its eyes . . .

"You've slept for a day and most of the night," Lady Savant said. "The sun will be up soon. We'll have breakfast, and maybe you'll feel like talking then."

Somewhere in her haze, Pram knew that she was being deceived. *Felix?* she called, but her mind's voice was small. Felix was gone. Felix was a lifetime ago. Clarence had drowned a lifetime ago.

Clarence. Pram thought of his blue eyes and his sad smile, and the tickets to Lady Savant's Spirit Show in his hand, and then the feel of his hand in hers. She could taste the chocolate-raspberry ice cream he'd bought her, and the haze thinned.

She thought of him and repeated his name over and over in her mind until her lips began to move. And Pram could see the dull yellow ribbons and the cracked tiles for what they were: unremarkable.

Lady Savant looked at Pram, and Pram stopped moving her lips. She did her best to look as though she were still entranced and that the dingy paisley wallpaper looked clean and new.

Behind them, the little girl stopped singing. Pram wanted to turn around and have a proper look at her, but she didn't want to let on that the girl was there. Lady Savant didn't seem to notice her.

At the end of the hallway there was a large kitchen, and a fire was burning in the woodstove. The room was large, and full of appliances that seemed rusted and old. There was a small table beside the woodstove that had already been set with two plates and two teacups, and a tray of desserts and glazed fruits.

Pram's stomach was rumbling, but she hesitated when Lady Savant pulled out a chair for her.

"It's okay," the little girl said, and hopped on top of the woodstove. "It isn't poisoned."

Pram sat. She was curious about this place, and she wanted to ask Lady Savant, but she had already resolved not to speak to her. Nothing good happened when she did. And so Pram silently pondered. This was surely not a house; it was large and drafty, and the kitchen looked like it belonged in a restaurant.

Lady Savant nudged the tray toward Pram, and Pram hesitantly retrieved a cookie. She took a bite, and it was one of the most delicious things she'd ever tasted, even though she no longer felt that she was dreaming.

Lady Savant clapped happily. Her pink nail polish was chipping, and she looked a bit older. Fine lines had taken root around her eyes.

How peculiar, Pram thought.

"This is my home," Lady Savant said. "You can stay for as long as you'd like. I know that we had discussed finding your father, but I've been thinking about that."

Pram set the cookie on her plate. Her hungry stomach had suddenly started to churn.

"Your mother came to me in another dream last night," Lady Savant said. "She told me that your father has made a new life for himself. He has a beautiful wife and a proper daughter."

Pram knew that Lady Savant was not to be trusted, and she didn't believe this. But the idea was enough to sadden her. If her father truly did have a proper family, it would mean that he had gotten over Lily and fallen in love with someone new. It meant he had a daughter who surely adored him, and there was no room for a reminder of something that had happened eleven years ago.

"Don't look so glum," Lady Savant said. "You can stay with me for as long as you like. I can give you something your aunts never could: I can show you how to reach the spirit world. I can make you the best spiritualist the world has ever seen, and one day you can use that skill to become a very wealthy woman."

If she were a wealthy woman, would her father want to meet her then? Pram wondered. She would have the money to sail across the ocean and find him on the other side of it, and he would see her at the helm and say that she took after him, with salt water in her veins, and they would have tea and it would be like they'd known each other all their lives.

The little girl with dark hair was humming, and she stopped just long enough to say, "Stay, stay."

The sun was starting to rise. The rusted appliances were gleaming.

Pram knew she didn't have a choice.

Lady Savant allowed the rest of their meal to carry on in merciful silence. Pram thought of Clarence every time she felt her mind going hazy again. She told herself, *If you're a ghost now, find me. You're always welcome wherever I am. Always.*

She thought of her aunts kissing her cheeks and telling her, "We love you." It had made her lips rise into a smile after they left the room.

They didn't mean it, Pram suddenly thought. The idea forced itself into her mind, as though it had been whispered in her ear.

Lady Savant smiled and poured a fresh round of tea.

CHAPTER 19

The building was very sad. Pram could tell that its rooms had once been filled with screams. Lady Savant walked her down the halls and asked her if she felt anything, and still, Pram didn't answer.

"This used to be a hospital," Finley said, suddenly walking beside her. "At least, I think that's what it was. I can't really remember."

Perhaps this was where he died from his burns. In Pram's experience, ghosts rarely wandered far from a place that had relevance to them—even if they couldn't remember what that relevance was.

She had met plenty of forgetful ghosts, but Finley had the worst memory by far.

They reached the end of the hallway, and Lady Savant

brought Pram up a rickety staircase that led to another
hallway that carried a different kind of sadness. Pram was
frightened to know that such a place could exist. Felix used
to tell her that if she let on about her abilities she could
end up at the circus, but he was wrong; there were worse
places one could go.

"Do you like your dress?" Lady Savant asked. "Brutus
made it for you."

Pram couldn't hide her surprise at the idea of
Brutus, the man with the thick arms, sewing a dress.

Lady Savant's smile was warm. "It's a talent of his," she
said.

It was absurd to think of that enormous man huddled
over a sewing machine. Pram would have laughed if she
weren't so unnerved by her ordeal.

"Lots of dresses," came a whisper in the wall. Pram
hugged her stomach and tried to warm herself against the
sudden chill.

Lady Savant could see that she was getting nowhere.
Pram, with that beautifully defiant face, was not ready to
trust her. She was quite stubborn, as Lady Savant knew
children could be. So she brought Pram back to her room
and said, "This morning has given you a lot to think about.
I'll get you when it's lunchtime." She closed the door behind
her as she left, and locked it.

The cage hung in the center of the room, the only thing

that resembled a bed. Its white silk blankets were rumpled, and in the daylight Pram could see that her sleep had been a fitful one. The wallpaper was pale green, like grass that was slowly browning during a drought, and covered with silver insects. The floor was chipped marble tile. Shadows of picture frames covered the empty walls. There was a dresser with chipping white paint and ceramic ballet slippers for handles; every drawer was empty.

The only window was barred from the outside, and beyond it, all Pram could see was an iron fence and some trees.

Pram walked the length of the room, dragging her fingertips along the wall. Unlike the restlessness and worry she'd felt lingering in the rest of this place, this room was eerily silent.

Pram sat on the floor, and her eyes began to fill with tears.

"Don't cry," the little girl with dark hair said. She played hopscotch on the tiles for a few seconds and then bounced to a stop. "It really isn't so bad here."

Pram swiped her wrist across her eyes. "I want to go home," Pram said.

"Oh, my, that is unfortunate," Finley said. He was perched on top of the cage like a bird. He slid down one of the bars and landed beside the girl with dark hair. "Lady

Savant doesn't lose her belongings, nor does she set them free."

"I don't belong to her," Pram said.

"But you do," the girl said. "Any living thing in this place belongs to her." She knelt before Pram and wiped at her tears. The tears fell through the girl's ghostly fingers, but Pram felt the warmth of the girl's touch, and for that she was grateful.

"What's your name?" Pram asked.

"Adelaide," the girl said.

"Did you die here?" Pram asked.

Adelaide shrugged. "I don't remember. Maybe."

"Am I going to die here?" Pram asked.

Adelaide's eyes widened. "No," she said. "The living things don't die here. They disappear."

"Disappear?" Pram said. Her palms were sweaty.

"One day we stop seeing them around," Finley said. "They start out in that cage, and they stay for a while, and then one day they're just . . . no more."

"How long has she been doing this?" Pram said.

Adelaide and Finley looked at each other and then back at Pram. "A long time," Adelaide said. "Maybe a hundred years. Maybe a million years."

"That's impossible," Pram said. "Lady Savant isn't old. Certainly not a hundred." She should have known better than to ask. Ghosts had a terrible sense of time. Felix used to say that they'd been friends for a hundred years, too.

"Isn't she?" Finley wondered aloud. "There was a girl in that cage before you, and a boy before that, and a woman once."

"Oh, yes," Adelaide said. "I liked her. She smelled nice."

"You're dead," Finley reminded her. "You can't smell anything."

"Well, she looked like she would smell nice," Adelaide said.

"Why were they here?" Pram asked.

"I can't remember," Finley said.

Adelaide shrugged. She had no cause to bother remembering such things, either. Memories were a way for the living to keep track of their lives, but for ghosts, there was no need to hold on to anything; Pram remembered an elder who had died, and his ghost stayed in the parlor for a week, reaching aimlessly into the jar of cough drops. When he was ready to go, he told Pram it was as though everyone and everything he'd ever known had been swallowed up by a cloud, and it was time to see what this cloud was all about.

Pram tried a different question. "Did the others have anything in common with me?"

Adelaide and Finley thought and thought.

"I forget," Finley said.

"Yes," Adelaide said. "They could see us."

Pram looked up at the cage; the lantern inside it still burned, casting shadows of bars on the walls, turning the entire room into a prison.

CHAPTER 20

The snow was like feathers. It wasn't cold, and Pram fell backward into it with a sigh.

One day an elder had let a stray cat into the house, and it tore through the pillow on Pram's bed, filling the room with feathers that floated in the air for days, despite Aunt Dee's furious vacuuming. This snow reminded Pram of that.

"It's lovely, isn't it?" Lady Savant said. "I thought we could have our lunch outside, sort of like a picnic." She laid a checkered blanket in the snow and set about unpacking the basket. Steam and the smell of fresh bread wafted toward Pram, whose stomach was growling again. It was hard to be stubborn when she was so hungry.

It was her third day with Lady Savant. At least, she

thought it was three. Her memory had become unreliable, just like her ability to reason dreams from reality. Thinking of Clarence still provided her with clarity, but her memory of him was becoming unreliable, too. She had been sure his hair was curly and light brown, the color of honey, but now she wondered if it had really been dark like oak, or blond like lemons.

And Felix was even blurrier. If she wanted to think of him, she had to first go back to a memory of one of the afternoons they'd spent lying in the sunlight, when his skin felt warm and real. But she was losing the sound of his voice, and with that, the things he'd said to her.

Finley and Adelaide were nice company, at least. Finley told jokes and sometimes danced and sang, and Adelaide played games. There were whispers in the wallpaper, old echoes in some of the rooms from ghosts who had long since moved on but left their thoughts behind. Pram talked to the echoes, and to Finley and Adelaide, and sometimes to herself.

But she was always silent around Lady Savant.

At first, Pram had thought silence was the best revenge against a woman who used her words against her, but Pram had overlooked something important: Lady Savant was the only living person Pram encountered—aside from the man with the thick arms, who never spoke to her and didn't seem to care whether she spoke to him. And though Finley and Adelaide were kind to her, Pram was lonely for conversation with someone from her own side, who still found relevance in the time of day. She missed the "Good mornings" and "Good nights." She missed "Have you done your lessons?" and "It's bath time."

Without these things to mark the hours, Pram was beginning to feel that she, too, was becoming a ghost.

And so she decided it was time to speak.

She said, "What time is it?"

Lady Savant, who was biting into a croissant, raised her eyebrows. She took a moment to chew and swallow daintily before looking at her wristwatch, which was gold. "It's quarter past noon."

Pram stuck out her tongue to catch a snowflake that fell all alone from the sky. "Thank you," she said. She also missed manners.

"You are most welcome," Lady Savant said. "Would you like some tea? I've brought a jar of honey."

Pram was hungry, and now at the mention of tea, her tongue longed for the taste of it. She nodded and crawled through the snow, bringing herself onto the picnic blanket. "Why am I not cold?" Pram said.

"Would you prefer to be cold?" Lady Savant asked.

Pram shook her head. Ever since the day the cat tore into her pillow, she'd wished real snow could be as warm and as soft, so that she could enjoy it without having to also endure a runny nose or red fingertips.

"Is this weather everything you've wished for?" Lady Savant said, as though she was reading Pram's mind. "It is cold, but you don't want to feel it, and so you don't. You're more powerful than you realize. I'd bet no one has ever told you that, because all that the world sees when it looks at you is a little girl."

Not everyone, Pram thought. There had been a boy and a ghost who saw something more when they looked at her, and she'd seen something extraordinary when she looked at them.

Their names escaped her, and after much furious thought, she remembered. Felix and Clarence. They'd left her. They didn't want her anymore.

No, that wasn't right—

"Try the tea," Lady Savant said.

Pram took a sip. It tasted like hot blackberry cobbler, unlike anything she'd ever experienced. She finished it in seconds.

"You've been seeing ghosts for as long as you can remember," Lady Savant said. "But it began with the insects, yes? And then people much later?"

Pram nodded. When she was eight years old, one of the elders read a chapter of *Alice's Adventures in Wonderland* to her each night before bed, and Pram had especially loved the Cheshire Cat, who was sometimes embodied as a mischievous grin. It had reminded her of the boy by the pond. *Felix*, she made herself remember.

"Seeing ghosts is only a small part of it," Lady Savant said. "As my protégé you'll learn how powerful you truly are."

Pram thought about the caravan ride a few days back, when she began to see the spirit world. "Can I go there?" Pram asked. "To where the ghosts are, I mean." She bit into a lemon scone.

"You can't stay there for a very long time," Lady Savant said. "Only for as long as you're able to hold your breath, and then you'll be pushed back into the living world. The spirit world knows who does and does not yet belong there."

Pram finished her scone and reached for another. She had never in her life been so hungry, and food had never been so delicious. She was sure she could never go back to regular oatmeal again without being disappointed.

Lady Savant smiled in a fond way, unlike the exasperated, worried smiles of Pram's aunts. And Pram wondered if this might be how a mother smiled at her child. She had no way of knowing.

"If I can't stay long, then what's the point?" Pram asked.

"It's a gift," Lady Savant said. "Don't you want it?"

Gift. Hadn't there once been a boy who told her she had a gift? She could no longer remember. "I've never thought of it as a gift," Pram said. "No one gave it to me. It's just the way I am."

"Oh, but that's where you're wrong," Lady Savant said. "You may have been an ordinary girl if only things had gone differently the day you were born."

"If my mother hadn't died, you mean?" Pram said.

"Yes," Lady Savant said. "Life and fate are fragile. Once things have happened, it's almost impossible to appreciate how easily they could have never happened."

Pram had thought about this. She wondered what it would have been like to have been born someone else entirely, or born a hundred years ago, or never born at all.

But there was one thing she wondered about more than all the rest. "Was my mother like this?"

Lady Savant's smile turned sad. "No, Pram. I'm sure she was ordinary. But that doesn't mean she didn't give you this gift."

Pram lowered one eyebrow in confusion. "I don't understand."

"No one has ever told you about your mother?" Lady Savant asked.

"Not very much," Pram said. "Her name was Lily and she liked to swim, and she died because of me. And she's unhappy with me for that."

"Is that what you think?" Lady Savant said.

"She must be," Pram said. "Why else would she come to you and not me?"

Pram could no longer remember what it was that Lady Savant had said about her mother's ghost. Her memory of that night was blurry. Many of her memories were blurry. She tried to think about the boy with the blue eyes (or were they brown?) and the ghost by the pond (or was he a fish that used to swim to her?), but the more she spoke to Lady Savant, the more distant these things seemed. The two-hundred-year-old colonial seemed farther away when she remembered looking at it from the tree by the pond. Had it been white? Yellow? Light blue? She had another sip of tea.

"Let's talk about something happier," Lady Savant said. "Have you ever been inside a memory before?"

Pram looked confused.

Lady Savant chuckled and took a bite of toast slathered with purple jam. She swallowed and said, "You can enter the memories of the dead. They don't mind. They've abandoned them. These memories float around in the air like balloons, not attached to anyone."

Pram looked up at the sky. The edges of clouds were

illuminated gold with sun. To know that the winter air was ripe with memories made her see the clouds differently, like flowers wanting to be picked.

"How?" Pram said.

"The more time you spend in the spirit world, the more they begin to appear."

Pram thought of the strange not-dream she'd had in the caravan after she entered the spirit world. She had been a girl with red hair, and someone had been calling her name, but she hadn't stayed long enough to hear what it was.

Was that someone's memory?

The idea delighted and worried Pram. "What if I got stuck?" she said.

"You can't," Lady Savant said. "If you were to enter the spirit world, it would be very possible to get lost. But you're entering a memory, and you can only stay for as long as you can hold your breath. Then you're forced back into the living world by your own desire to breathe."

Pram had had her fill of scones and tea, and now she drew a tree with jagged and bare branches in the snow. Trees had always saddened her, and at the same time reminded her of her mother, which was strange. Her mother spent time in the water, not in branches.

"How do I go back to the spirit world?" Pram asked.

Lady Savant was brushing the crumbs from the plates

and stacking them neatly in the basket. "All you have to do is want it," she said. "Anything you want is yours."

Pram was dimly aware of her body falling against the snow, her arms and legs crumpled like those of an abandoned marionette. And then in a second she forgot about her body entirely, and Pram disappeared.

She was a man in a hot air balloon, looking down at all the perfect green. From up high, the man thought, the world seemed so planned. Hunks of property fit together like puzzle pieces. The balloon drifted over a farm whose dirt had been combed by a giant rake, a red barn sitting to its left.

How very organized, the man thought. We really do belong here after all.

Pram awoke from the man's memory, gasping for air. Her eyes were watering as though she'd been in the kitchen while Aunt Dee was dicing onions.

Lady Savant wrapped the picnic blanket around Pram's shoulders. "Here," she said. "Your body is cold from the shock."

Pram felt dizzy, and it took nearly a minute for her to understand that her own body had never left the ground. Astonished, all she could say was, "I was floating."

Lady Savant looked worried.

But Pram wasn't worried at all. She could feel sweat pooling on her back and under her arms; her face was hot, and it was as if a light had just been turned on inside her, she thought.

She looked at the sky again. She had lived all her life never knowing what more she was capable of. Now that she knew, all she could think about was going back.

CHAPTER 21

For the next several nights, Pram lay in the gilded cage and concentrated on entering the spirit world.

Adelaide hopped around the room. "Come out and play," she said one night, after Pram had been still for a long while.

Pram opened her eyes. Without Lady Savant's help, she hadn't been successful in reaching the spirit world, and her head was beginning to hurt. "Adelaide," she said. "Why didn't you move on?"

Adelaide twirled and lifted up into the air before her skirt fanned out as she descended. "I was scared," she said. "I didn't think anyone would be waiting for me. I thought I could wait until my parents grew old and died, and then I'd go."

"So did they?" Pram said.

"I don't know," Adelaide said. "I don't remember them now. Or I guess I do, a little, but they're shadows." She pirouetted.

"Do you remember anything about being alive?" Pram asked. "Maybe I can find one of your memories. So far they've been random, but if I concentrate very hard, I might be able to find one that belongs to you."

Adelaide thought. She was quiet for such a long time that Pram sat up and looked for her to be sure she hadn't disappeared.

"Clickety-tapping," Adelaide said.

"Clickety-tapping?" Pram repeated.

"Yes," Adelaide said. "That sound." Her pale cheeks filled up with pink, and she smiled and continued twirling about the room, singing "clickety-tap, clickety-tap" and clucking her teeth.

Pram closed her eyes.

"You've worn yourself out," Finley said.

She gasped. He was forever appearing places, scaring her out of her wits. He clung to the outside of her cage and caused it to sway. "I've seen it happen before."

"Have you? When?" she said. She already knew his answer and she said it with him: "I can't remember."

"Well, I can't," he said.

"It was the others, silly," Adelaide told him. "All the others who lived in this room. Pram is just like them."

"I am not like them," Pram said. "I'm still here."

Adelaide said, "I hope you stay. I like you."

Stay. There was something wrong with that word, Pram thought, like the moment in her dream when she realized nothing she was seeing was real. "No," she said. "I can't stay. I have to go eventually."

"Go where?" Finley asked.

The door to the cage was open, and Pram stared through the space. She didn't answer right away, because she needed to concentrate so that she could remember. There was a feeling in her chest all of a sudden, a sense of urgency that was painful. Someone was waiting. A boy with blue eyes.

The hurt was unbearable, and Pram immediately forgot it.

"I don't remember," she said.

"Play with me," Adelaide said, holding out her hands and curling and uncurling her fingers.

"Okay," Pram said.

"Concentrate," Lady Savant said after an enormous dinner of candied yams and a turkey that was honey-glazed and almost too perfect to eat.

Pram concentrated.

"Think of something you want," Lady Savant said.

She was forever asking Pram for things she wanted, as though she could store a little girl's silly desires in glass bottles on a shelf.

But Pram didn't know what she wanted this evening. Dinner had been delicious, and she'd spent her afternoon playing in feather-soft snow and her nose hadn't run at all.

But when Finley tried to get her to climb a tree, she'd refused, and the feeling of fear was vaguely familiar. It wasn't the tree she had feared, but rather having to face the sadness those dead branches made her feel.

I want to know why I don't like trees, she thought, and closed her eyes.

She was a tall woman, and she was running, and sorrow was a heavy thing that she had swallowed. In her mind a compass was spinning. It was dizzyingly hot, and the woman had decided that the heat didn't matter. She no longer wished to dive into the cool ocean.

The woman did not think in words at all, but in broken kaleidoscope images. A boy's sweet grin, a crumpled letter, purple-pink lines like veins on stretching skin. It was furious and maddening and scary. It was exhausting, and it had been nineteen years like this. She didn't want to wait anymore. She was born waiting. A loop of a rope, a climb that scratched her palms as she went up the dogwood tree.

Her sisters would be livid if they saw her sitting up so high.

There was no need to take a deep breath. She dropped for the ground, knowing her feet wouldn't touch.

And then there was silence.

Pram did not open her eyes.

The man with the thick arms carried her to the cage.

Lady Savant paced and worried deep into the night. Adelaide and Finley paced behind her like ducklings. Lady Savant could not see them, but she sensed them. Every day, she could sense them a little more than the day prior. As Pram's memories began to fade, Lady Savant's began to return. Pram was exceptional, and far more powerful than the others had been. But she was the youngest yet, and now Lady Savant worried that she had pushed her too far too soon.

Pram was bright red with fever. Lady Savant reached into the cage and carefully, carefully pried one of her eyes open. As she had suspected, it was dull and dilated; her soul was not in the living world.

The man with the thick arms stood in the doorway, and the ghosts stopped pacing and watched him. "Is she dead?" he asked.

"No," Lady Savant said. "But I've never seen a living soul stay in the spirit world for so long before."

"I told you that you were pushing her too far," he said.

"She can stay in the spirit world longer than anyone I've seen. It's as though she has the ability to be living and dead at the same time. Miraculous."

Lady Savant brushed her fingertips across the child's sweaty forehead. Pram was her favorite, she'd decided. Not at all what she had suspected.

"I felt this one from the moment she stepped into the room, you know," Lady Savant said to the man with the thick arms. "I knew she was Lily's daughter. I followed her for a while just to be certain, and I was right. That ghost friend of hers made a tree fall right in front of me to scare me off, and that's when I knew she was something that even a ghost boy could see needed to be protected. I never would have guessed that hopeless girl could have such a remarkable child."

"Lily," Pram whispered, too softly for anyone to hear.

CHAPTER 22

Pram awoke with a feeling that her skin was too heavy. The moon was sliced into quarters by the bars on the window.

She took a deep breath just to be certain she was alive.

Adelaide was kneeling beside her. She had been petting Pram's cheek and whispering songs to her for most of the night. "Hello," she said.

"Hello," Pram said. Her voice was hoarse.

"Careful," Adelaide said. "You'll wake her."

Pram sat up and followed where Adelaide was pointing. Lady Savant slept at the bottom of the steps, her face in her arms.

"Has she been like that all night?" Pram asked.

Adelaide nodded. "She thought you were going to die. You haven't moved in a very long time."

"I'm scared," Pram whispered. "I think she's stealing my memories."

"She does like to take things," Adelaide said, and sighed. "I wish she wouldn't. It isn't right."

"I'd like to take them back," Pram said.

"You can't," Adelaide said.

Pram stared at the sleeping Lady Savant, and suddenly a feeling of anger returned to her. This woman had taken too much away. Pram didn't remember what those things were, but she still felt the loss.

"Maybe there is something I can get back," Pram said. "I entered a woman's memories before everything went dark, and in her mind there was a compass. I'm sure I remember it. If Lady Savant took it from me, I can reclaim it."

"A compass?" Finley said, appearing and sitting beside Adelaide. "Is that all you want?"

"It's the only thing I can think of," Pram said.

"If she took it from you, it's out in her caravan," Finley said. "That's where she keeps her treasures."

Pram stood as slowly as she could, trying not to make the cage's chain creak. This was the first time Lady Savant had left the bedroom door unlocked, and there would

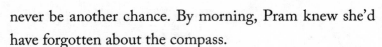

never be another chance. By morning, Pram knew she'd have forgotten about the compass.

She tiptoed down the steps and over Lady Savant's sleeping form. Lady Savant stirred and muttered something, and her eyelashes fluttered. Pram froze.

Adelaide knelt beside Lady Savant and sang:

While the moon her watch is keeping,
All through the night;
While the weary world is sleeping,
All through the night . . .

Lady Savant settled back into sleep. Adelaide kept singing.

"This way," Finley said. Pram opened the door just enough to slip through, and then she closed it.

"Can she hear Adelaide singing?" Pram asked.

"No," Finley said. "From what I've seen, Adelaide's singing just makes the living sleepy and they don't know why."

"I'm living and I can hear it," Pram said.

"Yes, but she likes you, so she lets you hear."

The hallway was full of screams and whispers. Nobody in this place could remember how they got here or what they were afraid of, but the building itself seemed to remember.

A firefly from the wallpaper in Pram's room had followed her, and as she walked it flitted and fluttered.

"Quiet," Finley warned. "Brutus is surely nearby."

They reached the end of the hallway, and there were two heavy-looking doors. Pram struggled to push one of them open, working against the cold that resisted her from the outside, as though it was warning her to stay.

Pram grunted and gave a final shove that opened the door. Flurries of snow were curling and swirling around the night air, and Pram had to run into them before the door closed behind her with a slam.

"I said 'quiet,'" Finley scolded.

"I couldn't help it," Pram said.

The poor firefly was trying to keep up with Pram, but the wind was knocking it about, making it fly in crooked circles.

"Where's the caravan?" Pram asked. Her voice was stolen by the wind. Her hair whipped to the left, as white as the snow itself, and Pram had a funny thought that she was disappearing. The wind was screaming a warning she couldn't understand.

Finley ran ahead of her. "Wait!" She chased after him. "Finley, wait!" She lost him in an instant, but she nearly ran headfirst into a building that appeared through the snow. She fell and picked herself back up and kept running.

At first she thought she had made her way back to Lady Savant's building, but no, this was some kind of a shed made of rickety wood. She felt along the wall until she found a door.

Inside, it was too dark to see. She didn't know what to do now; she was lost, and she wouldn't be able to find her way back to Lady Savant's building in this storm.

A sliver of light worked its way through. The firefly hovered an inch in front of Pram's face, and its light began to spread out until it reached all the corners of the shed. It had a dirt floor, and it was quite large for a shed. Pram thought it peculiar that she had never seen it, and that it didn't have a lock. Lady Savant's caravan sat square in the middle like a statue.

Finley appeared beside Pram. "Hello," he said.

"You left me," she said.

He shook his head. "I couldn't lead you here. You had to find it yourself."

"Why?" Pram asked.

"Because it's hidden," he said.

"No, it isn't, silly," Pram said. "It's right out in the open." She stepped forward and climbed into the back of the caravan. There were boxes and crates and trinkets that were covered by thick blankets.

Everything in this little caravan pulsed with the lives of those who had left them behind. "The dead hide pieces of themselves in the living world," Pram said to the firefly as it fluttered around her. "Did you know that?"

Pram dug through a box of things that clattered.

"What is it you said you were looking for?" Finley knelt beside her. "I'll help you find it."

Pram stopped rifling and blinked. What had she come here for? The image was just out of reach. "I can't remember."

"Can't have been too important," Finley said.

"No," she said. "It was very important."

She held up a necklace with a teddy bear charm, and then set it back down. She found an old lampshade with torn lace trim, and a gold wristwatch and a little doll with blue button eyes.

Something about that shade of blue filled her with pain.

She set the doll down and lifted a heavy blanket that had been covering a typewriter. She pressed down on one of its keys, and it sank below the other keys with a clicking sound, and then sprang back up. Pram pressed another key, and another. *Clickety-tap, clickety-tap.*

"I think this memory belongs to Adelaide," Pram said. One of the letter keys was loose—the *A*—and Pram put it in her pocket. She would give it to Adelaide when she returned. Maybe it would help her find her memories.

"Really?" Finley said, pushing one of the keys. "I wonder if anything here belongs to me."

They searched and searched, and Finley couldn't find anything that belonged to him, although he did find a Jacob's ladder that amused him.

"Did Lady Savant put this typewriter here?" Pram asked.

"Maybe, maybe not," Finley said. "When memories get abandoned, they have a way of drifting about until they accumulate with other memories. They don't like being lonely any more than people do, I guess."

Pram sat back and looked at the pile of things. She still hadn't found whatever she'd come here for, and they were out of places to look.

But then something caught Pram's eye. There was an empty crate resting against the caravan wall that she hadn't bothered to search. But now the firefly was hovering around it, and Pram caught a glint of metal between its slats. She reached for it.

"Did you find it?" Finley asked.

The glint of metal was attached to a chain. It was some kind of necklace. She dangled it before her face to get a better look. A compass.

Pram's mouth went dry. Time seemed to slow.

And then she was drifting away from the shore on a large ship. There was a girl at the water's edge with white-blond hair, standing on her tiptoes and waving to a sailor who watched her as the water pulled him back.

She was beautiful, even in the distance. She was a piece of the sun.

Pram gasped. "My father," she said, more to herself than to Finley or the firefly. "This belonged to my father. I found it in a box under the floorboards in my bedroom. I have—I have to get back home. My aunts will be worried about me."

Finley stopped playing with the Jacob's ladder and regarded Pram sadly. "It's too late for that," he said.

"No, it isn't," Pram said. "Why would you say that?" She hooked the compass around her neck and ran for the exit. When she threw open the door, the wind and snow were still raging, but the wind didn't disturb her hair or her clothes.

She looked straight ahead, and saw her body lying in the snow.

CHAPTER 23

"Wake up, wake up, *wake up*." Pram tried to jostle her lifeless body, but her hands moved right through it.

"It's too late," Finley said again. "I tried to tell you. Lady Savant hides her caravan where the living would never find it: in the spirit world."

"Don't say that!" Pram's voice cracked. "Look—I'm still breathing." She watched her own chest rise and fall. Her fingers and cheeks were blue.

"Barely breathing," Finley said.

"How do I go back to the living world?" Pram said.

"You can't," Finley said.

"I have to get Lady Savant," she said. "She won't let me die. She needs me. She says I'm her protégé."

"You wanted to run away from her," Finley said.

"Yes, well, I can't run anywhere if I'm frozen to death," Pram said. "I need for her to find me."

Pram ran through the snow with the firefly ever at her side, looking for the very building from which she'd run away just moments earlier. Or had it been hours? The wind was beginning to calm. Early-morning light crept between tree branches, turning them to veins against the gray sky.

"Being a ghost isn't so bad," Finley said, running alongside her. "I promise. We could be friends."

"We can be friends if I'm still alive," Pram said. "One of my best friends was a ghost."

Felix. His name returned to her, and it was as tangible as the compass around her neck. *Felix*, she thought with as much force as she could. *I won't forget you this time.*

They reached the building, and Pram stopped. "This isn't the right place," she said. The bricks were no longer weatherworn, but new and bright red. The snow was gone and there were flowers lining the perimeter.

She turned to Finley, but he was gone. Pram was distracted by a man who held a dying boy in his arms. "There was a fire a half mile up the road," the man called to another man in the building's doorway.

"You can't bring him in here," said the man in the doorway. "This is a hospital for the mentally unstable."

The men began to argue while the boy lay dying.

It was Finley.

"I'm in the past," Pram muttered to herself. But how far into the past?

She stepped through the hospital's front doors. The wallpaper was the same, but brighter and newer. And there were still screams coming from some of the rooms. To the left, in a room that Pram remembered to be closed off, there were people in wheelchairs or foldout chairs, some staring blankly and others sullenly playing games at foldout tables.

They muttered words that Pram couldn't understand. Were they speaking English? She moved closer to listen. None of them noticed. None of them looked up, and Pram could see that, even though some interacted with one another, they were each in their own little world.

Except for one nurse, that is, who knelt before a young woman's chair. Pram was drawn to the nurse like a moth to a flame, and when she got closer, she could see that the nurse was Lady Savant. But Lady Savant did not see Pram. Lady Savant was very focused on the woman in the chair.

"No one believes me," the woman in the chair whispered.

"I believe you," Lady Savant said. "I believe you do see the ghost in your coffee cup, and I'd like to help you."

Finley appeared beside Pram. "I remember that woman now," he said. "Shortly after I died, they closed this place down, but Lady Savant kept her here." As Finley spoke, the murmurs died down, and the bodies became transparent and then disappeared, and then the room was empty and covered in dust, and the wallpaper was old and faded.

"Why?"

"I don't remember," Finley said.

"Why must ghosts be so forgetful?" Pram said, more impatient than she'd ever been in her life. She was dying out in the snow and as she sought help, all she found were more mysteries.

"Why must the living worry about the past so?" Finley countered.

"Because it all means something when you're alive," Pram said, and ran past him, down the hall.

Adelaide came out of the bedroom and smiled brightly. "Oh, you're one of us now." She clapped. "Are you going to stay with Finley and me forever?"

"Adelaide, I've brought you something important," Pram said. She pulled the typewriter key from her pocket and held it out.

Adelaide squinted. "What is it?"

"It's a memory of yours," Pram said. "Clickety-tap."

Adelaide looked skeptical as she took the key and turned it in her hands. But then her eyes brightened, and she hugged her cupped hands to her chest and said, "My father."

"Yes?" Pram said.

"He was writing a novel," Adelaide said. "Oh, I remember now. He used to work on it after I'd gone to bed. And when I died, I was too afraid to move on, and so I stayed in my old bedroom for a long time. I wanted to wait at least until he'd finished it, so I could read how it ended. But he stopped writing after I died."

Her eyes filled with tears. Pram didn't know ghosts were able to cry.

"Thank you," Adelaide said. "I'd forgotten."

"You're welcome," Pram said. "I want to hear all about it later, but for now I have to find a way to wake Lady Savant. I'm going to die if she doesn't find my body."

Adelaide's teary eyes turned serious. Her mouth formed a nervous O. "What?" Pram said. "What's wrong?"

"I've just remembered something else," Adelaide said, and took Pram's hand. "Come on."

"There isn't time," Pram insisted.

"I know," Adelaide said. "But you don't want her to help you. I've just remembered that she did something terrible to the others." She tugged on Pram's wrist, and Pram had to run to keep up with her.

As they raced down the hall, the images in the wallpaper rattled. The screams in the empty rooms intensified; the wind picked up and pushed the tree branches against the windows. "What's happening?" Pram said.

"You're haunting the place," Adelaide said. "Your fear is doing it."

"How?" Pram said.

Adelaide stopped running and took Pram's hands. "In the living world, everything stays put until someone moves it," Adelaide said. "This is the spirit world. It changes from one moment to the next. Things happen here that the living can't see."

So this was Felix's world, Pram thought. He had tried to tell her that the spirit world was different from the living world, but he hadn't been able to describe it. Now she understood. No wonder he was afraid of leaving his tree by the pond.

"It's scary sometimes," Adelaide said sympathetically. She had her hand on a doorknob, and Pram found that she was dreading whatever awaited them on the other side of that door. Pram had never seen that door, and she suspected that Lady Savant had hidden it in the spirit world, just as she'd hidden her caravan, so that the living could never find it. "Stay close to me," Adelaide said, and opened the door.

There was a staircase that descended into a darkness that deepened with each step. "I haven't been here in a very long time," Adelaide said. "It scared me, so I forgot about it as quickly as I could. In the spirit world, if you forget about something, it's as though it never existed in your own mind."

"Until something reminds you," Pram said. "Like the typewriter key, or my father's compass."

"Yes," Adelaide said.

Finley had a terrible memory. There must have been a great many things he'd left behind, Pram supposed.

This staircase seemed to go on forever. By the time they reached the bottom, the smell of mold was overwhelming. In the spirit world, everything was intensified. "Where are we?" Pram asked.

"In the basement," Adelaide said.

The floor was dirt, and the walls were made of stones that were covered in grime. Somewhere, a pipe was drip, drip, dripping.

It felt as though they were walking forever. Pram worried about her body freezing to death out in the snow. "Adelaide, please, I don't have much time," she said.

"We're here," Adelaide said. "Look." She pointed to an old wooden shelf that was filled with mason jars. And though they resembled the ones Aunt Nan used to store her preserves, these were not ordinary jars, for each of them held ground dust in an array of colors that Pram had never seen. So strange were these colors that she didn't even have words for them.

"What is that stuff?" Pram asked.

"Ashes," Adelaide said. "That's what happens to souls when they're dying. Soon they'll be nothing."

Pram leaned close enough for the glow coming from the strange colors to touch her skin. "Lady Savant collects souls," she said, beginning to understand. She looked at Adelaide. "Is that what she wanted from me? My soul?"

"Not just any soul," Adelaide said. "All the souls she collected were from people who were like you and could see ghosts."

Pram was not in her living body, and therefore had no blood, but she was still sure she felt it go cold with fear. "What would she want with souls?"

"She uses them to stay young forever and to keep her powers," Adelaide said. "She drains them until they fade away to nothing, and then she finds more."

Pram looked at the jars with pity. She understood now what had been happening to her; she hadn't just been losing her memories the longer she stayed here; she had been losing her soul bit by bit as Lady Savant took it for herself.

"I think she stole my powers by getting me to talk to her," Pram said. "The more I said, the more she knew to take."

Pram ran her fingers over the lids. "Does one of these jars belong to me?" she asked. As though in answer, the jar she touched flashed with brightness. The color was not quite blue. It wasn't nearly as full as the others.

"That must be yours," Adelaide said. "Lady Savant has only managed to take a little bit so far."

Pram held the jar in her hands, and it beat like a heart, and it was very warm. She ran for the stairs, and Adelaide chased after her. "Pram! Where are you going?"

"To take this to my body," Pram said. "To wake myself up."

"How do you know that will work?" Adelaide said.

"I don't, but it's all I have," Pram said. "It has to work."

Finley was waiting for her at the top of the stairs, and he ran on one side of her while Adelaide ran on the other. "I didn't want to face that I was dead, either," he said.

"I'm not dead yet," Pram said.

"The living think the worst of death," Finley said. "But it isn't a punishment. It's just what comes next."

Pram stopped at the door. "Adelaide, can you keep singing to Lady Savant and make sure she stays asleep?"

"Will it help you save your soul?" Adelaide asked.

"Yes," Pram said. "It would help very much."

Adelaide smiled. She liked the idea that she could be useful. "Good," she said. "You have such a nice soul. It would be a shame for you to lose it."

Outside, gray-yellow sunlight was coming through the trees. Pram found her body easily—it was the only thing that dared to make a bed of this bitterly cold snow. She laid the jar beside her sleeping face, closed her eyes, and waited.

She opened one eye, and then the other.

"You're still a spirit," Finley said.

"Yes, thank you," Pram said.

Her sleeping face looked troubled, and Pram thought how frightening such a sight would seem to a living person who would find her that way. But from the spirit world, it didn't seem so troubling. The living world felt very far away and unimportant. Dying might not be as awful as she'd made it out to be.

No. She wasn't going to accept that. The spirit world had a way of making life seem trivial and distant, but she wouldn't succumb.

"Wake up!" she said.

Finley frowned. The way he stared down at her body was much like the way Pram's aunts stared at her mother's photo over the stairs, Pram thought, as though they were looking at a lost cause.

The sky began to growl, and the wind blew a dusting of snow right through Pram, who would have given anything to feel it on her skin. But her grief for the living world was cut short by the sight of Adelaide running toward her. Her hair flew behind her and her eyes were wide. "Lady Savant is coming for you," she cried.

"I thought your singing could make anyone sleep," Finley said.

"It can," Adelaide said. "Her body's asleep, but her spirit entered the spirit world."

If Pram had been able to haunt that hallway with her fears, Lady Savant had grown powerful enough to haunt the whole building and the space that surrounded it. The trees were bowing furiously, and the sun was drowning in black clouds. Lightning flashed. Pram felt a chill in her bodiless soul.

"Run," Adelaide and Finley said.

But Pram didn't.

"I remember now," Finley said. "Once Lady Savant has gathered enough power from a new soul, she gets stronger. She was beginning to weaken until she found you. You've been replenishing her."

The ghostly wind was blowing their hair from their eyes. "Yes, I know that now," Pram said. "I wish you'd remembered that much sooner."

Lady Savant's spirit broke through the closed doors of the building, and the way she ran was unnatural, floating above the ground as she was. She was twice as tall and surrounded by whispers and screams.

Pram forced herself to stand up straight, fists clenched at her sides.

Lady Savant's features changed from one instant to the next. Her hands belonged to a woman, and then a child, and then a woman again. Her eyes were dark and then light. Her hair was wild and streaked with silver. For a second her skull showed through her skin.

When Lady Savant spoke, it came out as a windy howl. "What have you done?" she said.

Pram had seen dozens of spirits, but none like this. Lady Savant was not an ordinary soul, but rather a revolving assortment of every soul she had ever stolen.

"I'm dying," Pram said, impressed with the bravery in her voice. "I was running, and I must have gotten tired and collapsed in the snow."

Lady Savant swirled around her. A voice in her billowing sleeves begged for help.

"This won't do," Lady Savant said. "I needed you alive for much longer." She stooped to pick up the jar with Pram's glowing soul, but Pram grabbed it first. She hugged it to her chest and stepped back. It was beating like a heart against her. *Thump-thump, thump-thump.*

Finley stepped in front of her.

Lady Savant's eyes flashed something dangerous. "You again," she said. "It's been a long time since I was able to see you. I'd hoped you and that peculiar little girl had moved on by now."

"I won't let you take her soul," Finley said. "It's too good for you."

"You've always been a meddlesome ghost," Lady Savant said.

"Pram, run," Finley said.

"I can't," Pram said.

"This is no time to be stubborn."

Pram looked at the iron gate that had confined her when she was a part of the living world. Even if she could break through it now as a spirit, what good would it do? No one in the living world would be able to hear her.

The needle of the compass spun around and around. It didn't know where to go, either, Pram thought.

Lady Savant grabbed Pram's shoulders. She had the burly hands of a man, and then the hands of an infant, and then a pianist's fingers, but her grasp never weakened.

Pram had never felt pain like this. Though her body and its skin and bones lay in the snow before her, she could feel a stinging in her blood like bees. Lady Savant opened her mouth and it became as wide as a cave, and it was filled with howling winds.

This is it, Pram thought. *She's going to swallow me whole.* But she couldn't move, not even to catch the jar as it fell from her hands.

Adelaide sang. Her voice was harried and loud and desperate, but Lady Savant could not be lulled to sleep this time.

Pram's eyes began to close, and her feet faded from under her. Her body, in the snow, let out a wounded whimper as her lungs started to slow.

She knew that her soul was being stolen and she was disappearing, and with her remaining strength, her mind could only muster one word; it was the first thing she ever said when she was afraid.

Felix . . .

Heat lapped at her skin, and Pram opened her eyes to find that Lady Savant and the snowy field were gone. She was standing in smoke and flames. No, crawling. She was a boy and she had spilled the lantern in the hay and couldn't find the way to the door. She knew that the horses were dying. She could hear them stomping and screaming as they burned.

"I've got you," a voice said. Hands under her arms pulling her through the hay and dirt.

"Finley." She coughed. "I don't understand."

"I didn't want to remember this day," Finley said. His jaw was tight, and Pram, as a boy, knew that she was his brother. She knew her name, too.

Felix. This was the memory of his death. She and Finley were playing it out.

A burning rafter fell from the ceiling, and it was meant to kill her, but Finley had lived this day once before, and this time he was prepared. He pulled Pram the boy out of the way and kicked the barn door open.

Finley and Pram spilled out into the snow. Finley was still a spirit, but Pram was a living girl, and she crawled onto her hands and knees, spluttering frozen air.

Lady Savant was gone.

"What happened?" Pram was shivering now.

"Finley dived in after you," Adelaide said. "Lady Savant was forced back into the living world. But you have to leave before she comes for you. Can you walk?"

Pram wanted to leave more than anything, but her eyes wouldn't stay open, and as much as she tried to cling to her body, she fell back into the spirit world.

CHAPTER 24

The police car stopped at the iron gate that surrounded the abandoned building. The officer couldn't be sure what had persuaded him to turn down this icy back road; he could only be sure that the notion had been so strong it was as though a pair of hands had turned his steering wheel for him. He couldn't know that notion was really the ghost of a boy who had died decades before.

There was nothing here, save for an old institution that had closed more than a century ago and was rumored to be haunted. The police in this town encouraged these rumors because it kept children from sneaking onto the property to play or to damage it.

Which was why it was especially surprising when the officer saw a girl lying in the snow.

Adelaide clutched her typewriter key and looked like she was trying not to cry. She had sung until Lady Savant's snoring rattled the floorboards; she wanted to be sure the police would hear the snores.

"Are you going back to the living world?" Adelaide asked.

"I hope so," Pram said, watching as the officer felt for her body's pulse and wrapped her body in his coat.

"We'll miss you," Finley said. "I suppose you won't be back to visit us."

"You can visit me," Pram said. Her voice felt softer, like it was fading.

"How will we know where to find you?" Adelaide said.

"Yes, we're ghosts, not psychics," Finley said.

Pram smiled at the pair of them and wrapped them in a hug. "It's a two-hundred-year-old colonial. It's white. There's a tree and a pond in front." She thought of Felix when she mentioned his tree, and a bit of that old pain returned. "Come and haunt me anytime you like."

Adelaide turned the typewriter key over and over in her fingers. "I have a lot of thinking to do," she said. "Now that I remember my parents, I miss them, and I'm sure they're waiting for me. Jacob and Madeleine Pierce." She said their names a few more times, handling them like precious things that had been stolen and returned to her.

"Would you like me to help you?" Pram said. "I'm not sure how it works, but I could try."

Adelaide hesitated.

"What would be the point in moving on?" Finley said. "Everything is perfect right here."

Pram's head was light, and she felt very weak. She knew that her time in the spirit world was ending.

She grabbed Finley's hands. "Follow me back home if you'd like to see Felix again. I don't know for sure whether he's moved on. He hasn't answered me in a long time. But if he turns up again, I'm sure he'd remember if he saw you."

Finley shook his head. "He's forgotten what happened. It's for the best that I go back to forgetting, too." He tried to smile. "But you'll look after him?"

"I promise," Pram said.

Adelaide waved. She was so far away. "Bye," she and Finley were saying. "Bye, Pram, we'll miss you!"

The jar that held Pram's soul shattered and then disappeared.

Miles and miles away, in a two-hundred-year-old colonial house, a phone rang just as the teakettle whistled. In the past week, Aunt Dee and Aunt Nan had become afraid of the phone and what sort of news might be on the other end of its line. One of the aunts answered while the other stood twisting its cord in her anxious fingers. Even the elders went silent.

And then Aunt Dee sagged with relief. "Yes," she said. "Yes, we'll be right there."

As Pram drifted somewhere between the spirit and the living worlds, she entered another memory.

This time she was Lady Savant. She wore a nurse's uniform and pushed a cart full of little cups that held pills—yellow, red, blue. There were dozens of institutions like this, and Lady Savant had seen many of them. They were the perfect place to find extraordinary souls hiding among the hopeless and the delusional.

Lily was both hopeless and delusional, and not at all what Lady Savant needed. Lily was plain and Lily could not see ghosts, and she spent her days sitting by the window, staring out at the dogwood tree as though it was her precious sailor who had left her behind.

And now, Lily was pregnant. Her spinster sisters had brought her here in hopes that the rest would do her some good. And undoubtedly the baby she birthed would be equally plain and equally hopeless, Lady Savant thought.

"Would you like something to drink?" Lady Savant asked her.

"I think I'd like to take a walk," Lily said.

"Too hot for a walk in your condition," Lady Savant said.

Lily stared at her stomach as though she'd forgotten the baby was there at all. Her sadness tasted like rusted metal on Lady Savant's tongue. And though Lily was ordinary, that sadness was profound.

"You're not a real nurse. You can't stop me," Lily said, and went back to staring at the dogwood tree.

Pram felt the memory ending, no matter how she fought to hang on to it.

"Wake up," a voice said. "You've been gone for too long already, you silly girl."

The voice filled her with so much hope that it pushed her back into the living world, where hope was more precious than gold. It was a voice she hadn't heard in a very long time, and one she had missed desperately.

"Felix," she answered him. It was little more than a whisper. She felt a hand stroking her cheek, and she opened her eyes expecting to see Felix. But Aunt Dee and Aunt Nan were the ones standing over her.

"Pram?" they said.

Pram's voice was hoarse. "Where am I?" she said.

Aunt Nan kissed Pram's hand. There were tears in her eyes. "You're in a hospital, but you're all right now. The Blue boy told the police everything. The whole town's been looking for you."

Pram's heart was beating in both her ears. "Clarence?" she said. "He's okay?"

"You've gotten her too excited," Aunt Dee said.

Pram tried to sit upright, but they held her shoulders. "There will be time for all that later," Aunt Dee said. "You're recovering from pneumonia."

"I feel all right now," Pram said, which was only a little bit true. "Tell me about Clarence? Please?"

"He's been by to see you every day," Aunt Nan said, and sighed like she thought this was romantic. "He told us about that madwoman who kidnapped the two of you."

"The police can deal with her now," Aunt Dee said. "Her and that man she was with. Lord knows what was going through their minds, living in an abandoned asylum."

"She was a spiritualist," Pram said.

"We don't have to talk about this now," Aunt Dee said, tucking Pram's hair behind her ears. "You just worry about getting well."

"She said she'd spoken with my mother," Pram said. The aunts paled. "So you see, it's all my fault," Pram said. "I believed her."

"What did she say about your mother?" Aunt Nan asked. Aunt Dee elbowed her and glared.

"She said my mother could tell me where my father is," Pram said. She had kept it a secret that she wanted to find her father, but now she was tired of holding on to secrets.

The aunts exchanged hesitant expressions. And then Aunt Dee said, "You never asked about your father before."

Pram's eyes began to fill with tears as she spoke. "Clarence's mother died, so we went to a spiritualist to try to find her. Then we both thought that if his mother was lost forever, at least we could find my father because he was still out there somewhere."

"That's an awful big undertaking for two children," Aunt Dee said, wiping her misty eyes. "Honestly, Pram, we had no idea."

Pram sobbed. It wasn't just that she hadn't found her father, but also the memory of her mother sitting in that asylum while Lady Savant handed out pills, and Felix disappearing, and Clarence being left to drown in that lake, and all the souls that died in those jars. It was over now, all of it, and Pram very much needed a good cry.

The aunts couldn't bear it. They cried, too, and they held her hands and kissed her cheeks, and they thanked whatever god sat in the heavens that she had come back to them.

CHAPTER
25

Pram wasn't allowed to have a proper visit with Clarence as long as she was in the hospital. Every day for the rest of that week, he brought her a flower he'd folded in that day's newspaper, and the aunts stayed in the room and made sure that Pram did not discuss The Madwoman Incident—as it had come to be called. So Clarence told her about what she was missing in school and how chilly it was outside, and Pram could see in his eyes that there was more he wanted to say. He could see it in her eyes, too.

The first moment Clarence and Pram had alone was the day she returned home. She was sitting in her bed, rereading *A Midsummer Night's Dream*, and he appeared in her doorway, holding a tray of soup and toast. "Your aunts asked me to bring you your lunch," he said.

The moment he set the tray on Pram's desk, Pram threw her arms around him. "I thought you drowned," she said.

"I thought you were gone forever," Clarence said, hugging back with just as much gratitude.

After a very long time, Pram stepped back and looked at him. "How did you get out of the crate?"

"I didn't," Clarence said. "I tried to open it, but it was nailed shut. The water was very murky and it was dark."

Pram's chest felt tight.

"And then a boy swam down to me, and the crate broke apart, as though it wasn't nailed at all, and the boy brought me to the surface. I think I blacked out after that. He wasn't there when I woke up."

"What did he look like?" Pram asked.

Clarence thought. "It's kind of fuzzy, but . . . he had dark hair. And he was wearing a ripped white shirt, and he was skinny, and I know this sounds silly, but he glared at me as though I was getting on his nerves."

Pram was smiling. "You saw Felix."

Clarence blinked. "I did?"

"You must have been dying," Pram said. "That's the only explanation."

"I read about that happening," Clarence said. "Sometimes a near-death experience can make one see a ghost. It had me considering some foolish things when I was looking for my mother's ghost."

"Have you seen any other ghosts since?" Pram said.

"Not a one," Clarence said. "I'm back to being ordinary, I guess."

"I don't think you're ordinary at all," Pram said. "And I'm glad you're alive."

"I'm glad you're alive, too," he said. "I didn't know what Lady Savant was planning. I didn't think I'd ever see you again."

"You almost didn't," Pram said. She closed her door, and in a hushed tone, she told him everything.

"And you haven't heard from Felix except for that one time when you were waking up at the hospital?" Clarence said.

"No." Pram frowned. "And I don't know if it was really even him, or just a dream."

"But I saw him in the lake," Clarence said. "So that must mean Lady Savant didn't help him to move on after all."

"Adelaide told me that no one can help a spirit move on," Pram said. "It has to be their own idea. But Lady Savant must have done *something* to keep him from reaching me."

"To keep him from warning you about her," Clarence said.

Pram chewed on her bottom lip. "Maybe," she said.

"Clarence!" Aunt Dee called from the bottom of the stairs. "Your father is here to take you home."

Pram opened her door and looked out over the banister. "But he just got here," she said.

"You should be in bed eating your lunch," Aunt Dee said. "Your friend can come and visit another time."

"It's okay," Clarence said. "Feel better, Pram. I'll come back tomorrow."

Before he went downstairs, he whispered, "And Felix will turn up."

After Clarence had left, Pram ate her lunch and climbed back into bed to finish reading her play.

Aunt Dee knocked on the open door. "May I come in?" she asked.

It was strange of her to ask, Pram thought, but she set down her book and said, "Of course."

"I thought we could have a little talk, you and me," Aunt Dee said, and sat on the edge of the bed. She was holding Pram's father's compass. "They found this in the snow beside you," she said. "I'd like to know where you got it."

Pram hesitated. She had never told her aunts about the box of things her mother hid in the closet floorboard. "May I have it back, please?" is all she said.

Aunt Dee stared at the compass as though it might speak to her. "It's been twelve years since I've seen this," she said. "Your mother wore it all around the house, as though it was the thing telling her where to go with every step. I thought it was lost for good."

Pram looked at the compass, too, wishing she could connect it to a real memory. Before Pram met Lady Savant, all the memories she'd had of her mother were make-believe, and no matter how real they might have seemed, her mother would always be a stranger who knew nothing about her at all.

"Your aunt Nan and I have wanted to protect you from the truth about your parents," she said. "But we may have done the wrong thing. Neither of us had any idea you gave them so much thought."

"I thought it would make you mad if I asked about my mother," Pram said.

"Why would we be mad?" Aunt Dee asked.

"Because she died giving birth to me, and it's all my fault," Pram said, guilt knotting her stomach. "And you've both had to raise me. I thought that I was old enough to find out for myself where I really belonged."

"Oh, Pram, no," Aunt Dee said. "It's not your fault at all."

"We wanted to raise you," Aunt Nan said. She was standing in the doorway, dabbing at her misty eyes with a handkerchief; she'd been weeping a lot since Pram's return. "We had the adoption papers filled out and waiting before you were born."

Aunt Dee glared. "Don't tell her the whole truth," she said. "She's too young yet."

"She deserves to know," Aunt Nan cried. "After all the poor child has been through." She sat on the other side of Pram's bed and cupped Pram's face in her hands. "I don't want you to think for one second that you weren't welcome here."

Pram's eyes hurt with the threat of tears. "But I killed your sister," she said.

"Is that what you think?" Aunt Nan said. "Pram, your mother—"

"Don't you dare tell her that part," Aunt Dee snapped.

"Your mother was very ill," Aunt Nan said pointedly. "As you grew up, your aunt Dee and I wanted you to have a nice image of her, and so we told you all the good things. We told you she liked to read, and that she was a good swimmer, and we kept that picture above the stairs because it's the only truly happy photo of her. But that wasn't everything, and you have a right to know that. Toward the end, before you were born, she was living in a special hospital."

"An asylum," Pram said, to prove that she knew the word. She knew more than she usually let on.

"Yes," Aunt Nan said. "The truth is that your mother was a very sad girl. She died on the day you were born, but you weren't the thing that killed her, and I won't have you go on thinking you're to blame. Someday when you're older, we'll tell you the rest of it, but for now all you need to know is that she had always been sad, and she spent much of her life in and out of . . . hospitals. Your aunt Dee and I knew she wouldn't have been able to take care of you. Your mother knew it, too, and we all agreed that it would be best if you were here with us."

"What about my father?" Pram said.

Aunt Dee looked like she was going to say something unkind. She opened her mouth and then shut it.

Pram's shoulders dropped. "He didn't want me," she said. "Did he?"

Aunt Nan frowned and fussed with Pram's hair. "He sends money for your upbringing sometimes. Never any letters."

Pram stared at the compass, which was then swallowed by Aunt Dee's fist. "She's too young to be hearing this," Aunt Dee said.

"Clearly she isn't too young if she's old enough to be asking about it," Aunt Nan said.

"I needed to hear the truth," Pram said, her voice weak, as though she'd been punched in the stomach. "Thank you."

"We're sorry, Pram," Aunt Nan said. "Really, we are. If we'd had any idea how much you wanted to meet him—"

"I wanted to know the truth about him," Pram said. "I wanted to know what he was like, and if he knew about me. That's all, I guess."

She still wanted to meet him, but knowing that he knew where she lived all her life, and hadn't wanted to visit, lessened her desire. Perhaps one day, she thought, when she was older. Maybe they would both be different people then.

Aunt Dee threw the compass at the wall. It bounced back and hit the floor. Pram and Aunt Nan winced. "If you want to know the truth about your father, he never deserved you," Aunt Dee said. "He was like a fly that got into the house. Once he met your mother, there was no being rid of him. He'd breeze into town on his little visits from wherever he'd been, and he'd sweep your mother off her feet and get her hopes up, and then he'd leave once he'd had his fun."

I see your exquisite face at every port. I've made a horrible mistake leaving you behind. Forgive me, forgive me, forgive me.

"But he loved her," Pram said. All those beautiful letters in that box in the closet, none of them for her.

"Maybe he did," Aunt Nan said sympathetically. "But he was a nomad and there wasn't enough room in his life for Lily, or for you."

Pram stared at the closet door as though her father would somehow emerge from his letters and speak for himself.

"If you'd like to meet him, maybe we can arrange something," Aunt Nan said. "I have a PO Box address. You could write him a letter."

"No," Pram whispered, still reeling from all the revelations. "Not now, anyway."

"Can we get you anything?" Aunt Nan said. "Would you like some cake? I think I'll bake you a cake. Dee, do we have any eggs left?"

"You can't give her something that'll rot her teeth every time she's unhappy," Aunt Dee said.

As her aunts argued about whether the cake was a sensible decision, Pram stared at the compass that lay on the floor. It no longer meant what she had thought it meant. All that trouble to find him, and he knew where she was; he just didn't want to visit.

"I don't want cake," Pram said suddenly. "And I don't want to write my father a letter. I want to go back to school on Monday."

"School?" Aunt Dee said.

"You wanted to protect my mother, didn't you?" Pram said.

"More than anything," Aunt Nan said. "We tried everything. The best hospitals. Home care. Chicken soup."

"And you've tried to protect me," Pram said. "But I don't want to hide anymore. I'd like to spend more time in the living world. I don't think I need to be protected the way that my mother did."

Aunt Dee smiled sadly. "No, I suppose you don't," she said. "It startles me how much you look like her, but you've never been Lily. You've always been Pram."

"Our pragmatic niece," Aunt Nan said.

Just as the compass seemed different to Pram now, so did the aunts. Pram looked at them and realized how wrong she'd been. All that trouble to find where she belonged, and it had always been here.

That night, Pram couldn't sleep. She stared at the silhouettes of tree branches on her wall, and she thought of Lady Savant and of her mother, whose paths had only briefly crossed.

She felt the pull of a memory drawing her in, and then her bedroom disappeared, and she was a nurse in a room that stank of mold and metal. The rooms behind her were filled with screams, but the commotion had long faded into a distant malaise. She had learned not to pay it any mind, even when it haunted her dreams.

Instead, the nurse focused on the metal tray in her hands, most notably the slender S-shaped utensil that the doctor retrieved. There had been much debate in the field about using it on such a young patient as the girl before them, but the girl's parents were desperate and they'd agreed.

The girl was bound to her mattress. Earlier she had been kicking and flailing, but now she was weary, and her hands flinched like fish dying on the shore. Her eyes were big and dark and bloodshot from old tears. She saw the S-shaped tool and whimpered.

"It's going to be all right now, Claudette," the doctor said, and pressed his palm to her forehead, steadying her. "We're going to make the ghosts go away now."

Pram forced herself out of the memory. Her cheeks were wet with tears.

"I'm sorry they hurt you," she whispered to Lady Savant, even though Lady Savant could not hear her.

CHAPTER
26

Pram was wearing three scarves, a pair of mittens, and a sweater underneath her coat. Her aunts insisted that every one of these things was necessary if she was to go outside, even though most of the snow had melted.

The pond was no longer frozen. Pram walked to its edge, but all she saw when she tried to peer into the water was the sky's reflection.

"Felix?" she said. "I don't know if you can hear me, but I wanted to say thank you. For saving Clarence. I know you were always a bit jealous of him."

"I am not jealous," Felix said. Pram followed his voice and found him sitting up in his tree. "He has a funny-looking nose, and eyes like a Saint Bernard's."

"Felix!" Pram jumped excitedly. "Where have you been?"

"That's a fine question, and I don't know the answer," he said, hopping to the ground in front of her. "That batty woman hypnotized you in the middle of the night and forced you to tell her all your secrets. Once you were back in bed and safe again, I was so angry about the whole thing that I went to give her a good old-fashioned haunting— rattling the windows and giving her gooseflesh and everything.

"And then, next thing I knew, I was trapped in someone else's memories. And when I found my way out, I was thrown right back into someone *else's* memory. And so on. The most pointless things like ballroom dances and car rides. At one point I believe I was trapped in your wallpaper, making the petals move."

"Lady Savant is very dangerous," Pram said.

"I thought I'd be trapped like that forever," Felix said. "I was beginning to forget who I was. And then I heard you screaming. 'Felix! Felix!' You were so loud that I found my way back just in time to watch that batty woman throw your boyfriend into the lake."

"Clarence isn't my boyfriend," Pram said flatly.

"Not yet," Felix said.

Pram blushed.

"Anyway, after I dragged him out of the lake, you were long gone. I tried to find you, but it was as though you'd stopped existing."

"Maybe Lady Savant blocked you from hearing me," Pram said.

"I was worried," Felix said. "I didn't know where you could be. So I waited here, and I thought that if you died, your spirit would come back here and find me."

"I did enter the spirit world for a little while," Pram said. "My body was lying in the snow."

"I'm glad you're alive," Felix said. "I prefer you this way."

"I'm happy about it, too," Pram said. "Lady Savant was teaching me to reach your world, the spirit world, but I don't think I want to do it anymore."

"Really?" Felix said. "Not at all?"

"Well, maybe. But only if I can help someone," Pram said. "I'm becoming quite good at recovering memories. I've even been able to enter the memories of the living sometimes. I could try to help you remember who you were, if you want." She didn't tell him what she already knew; she would tell him if he ever asked, but it would have to be his decision.

Felix shook his head. "I forgot those things for a reason," he said.

Pram supposed this was true. He had died as a child, after all. "I've missed you," she said. "Why didn't you visit me right when I came back?"

"I did, here and there when you were asleep," Felix said. "But I left before you woke up. I thought it was important for you to be among the living while you got better."

Pram smiled. How selfless and incredibly sweet of him. "I'm better now," she said.

"Yes," Felix said. "Except for that strange lump on your ear."

"What?" Pram said.

Felix reached toward her ear, but then swiped the hat from her head and took off running.

"Hey!" She laughed and chased after him.

From the window of the two-hundred-year-old colonial, Aunt Dee and Aunt Nan watched Pram play with her invisible friend. "Let her have her fun," Aunt Dee said. "She'll only be a little girl for so long."

Pram spent most of the afternoon playing with Felix. They built a rather pitiful creature from the dregs of snow still on the ground and decided he was a banker with two bad legs and a permanent scowl.

"I like him anyway," Pram said.

"Yes, me, too," Felix said, laughing. "Even though he looks more dead than me."

Pram smirked.

"I wish it could be like this forever," Felix said. He sounded sad, and Pram looked at him with concern. "I've been doing a lot of thinking while you were away," he said. "It felt like you were gone for a thousand years, and I began to think that I should just move on. You're the only thing left for me in this world anyway."

"I'm back now," Pram reminded him.

"You didn't wake up for a long time," Felix said. "And I wondered if you would die, and come meet me in the spirit world and be a girl forever. But then I thought about how clever you are and how much your aunts and that boy care about you, and I knew that you belonged in the living world. So I told you to wake up."

"I remember that," Pram said. "I knew that was you."

"You are going to be a very interesting grown-up one day, Pram. You'll do lots of things. You'll help people, both living and dead. You'll have a daughter named Felix, and I'll meet her on the other side after she's lived to be a hundred and moved on. It's not fair for me to try to keep you coming back to see me. I need to let you grow up."

"I don't need to grow up today," Pram said. She grabbed his hand.

"Soon," Felix said. "I think I'm ready to go soon." But when Pram rested her head on his shoulder, for one self-ish moment he wished that he really could keep her for the rest of time.

CHAPTER 27

In the nights that followed, Pram could not forget the memory she'd visited, in which Lady Savant had been a little girl and the doctors in the asylum held her down.

There was a lot of bad in Lady Savant, but she had not started out that way. Pram was sure of that. She would lie awake in bed and think of the things Lady Savant had taught her. Lady Savant had not been an especially honest woman, but Pram believed there was truth to many of the things she'd said.

One particular night, unable to sleep, Pram climbed out of bed, turned on her desk lamp, and made a list of things she had learned while in Lady Savant's asylum:

It's a gift.
Talking to Lady Savant makes me lose my memories.
Thinking of Clarence helps me to remember.
Memories of the dead float like balloons.
All I have to do is want it. Anything I want is mine.

Pram sat in the oval of light from her lamp for a long while, thinking of all the memories that drifted through the air. As far as she understood, the memories were not something she could control. She might enter the memory of a child on a swing or a man in a hot air balloon. Or she might enter a dark memory, a last memory—one that might well break her heart. Pram decided she wasn't willing to take that chance. Not tonight, at least.

This didn't mean that she didn't want answers. Though Pram had tried to appease her aunts and behave like a normal child, Lady Savant had shown her that she did in fact have a gift. The spiritualist hadn't said that Pram was strange— she'd said she had a gift. And Pram was grateful for that. She knew that it would stay with her for the rest of her life.

"She tried to steal my soul," Pram reasoned during lunch. "She was only using me so she could keep her youth and gain my powers."

Clarence frowned. "You don't sound convinced."

Pram took a bite of her sandwich. After a moment, she said, "Do you think it's strange that I'm grateful to her?"

"My mother used to say that there's a reason for everyone we meet," Clarence said. "Everyone impacts us in some way or other."

It didn't answer her question, but Pram knew it was the best answer anyone could give her. She began folding her napkin into squares and then triangles, losing herself in worry and thought, until Clarence said, "Maybe what you need is closure."

Pram nodded. "I think I need to see her one last time. I don't know what I expect exactly; I just feel as though there's something she needs to show me. One last something."

Clarence was worried. "The last time you felt you needed to see her, it was a trap. She lured you while you were asleep."

"I've thought about that," Pram said. "I've been writing down my dreams. I started shortly after I came back home. Nothing has been unusual about them. And I think Felix would sense if something wasn't right."

"What does Felix think of you seeing Lady Savant again?"

Pram sank between her shoulders. "I haven't told him."

"Oh," said Clarence, and Pram knew he was surprised

that she'd shared a secret with him and not with Felix as well. He was gracious enough not to smile about it, though.

"When I was with Lady Savant and she was stealing my memories, the only thing that seemed to bring me back was you," Pram said, and her cheeks felt very hot. "I think—if you were to come with me . . . I think I would be okay."

Clarence was looking at the table. Pram glanced at him and saw his smile.

Pram and Clarence decided it would be best not to tell Pram's aunts about visiting Lady Savant. They had agreed to let their niece attend school, but they were still hesitant to relinquish her into the world. Aunt Nan was only just starting to recover from her frenzy of nervous baking; the elders had enjoyed the post-dinner treats, but they were often out of eggs and butter, and Aunt Dee had been forced to hold an intervention.

"We're going to the library," Clarence told them after he and Pram returned from school. They would be sure to stop by the library so it wouldn't be a lie. Pram felt horribly guilty about the whole thing, and so Clarence did all the talking.

"Be back for dinner at six thirty," Aunt Dee said. Pram gnawed on her lip and nodded.

As she and Clarence walked away from the house, Pram could feel her aunts watching her from the window.

"Is Felix here?" Clarence asked as they passed by the pond.

"No," Pram said. "I'm not sure where he's gone." Felix had taken to wandering lately. He had followed Pram to school once. He perched on the curtain rod and listened to the teacher talk about the continents. He roamed the halls and found the older children having an art class, and he looked over their shoulders as they painted cryptic hints about their lives. It made him curious about other classrooms, and then other buildings, and other towns entirely.

He had gotten very brave. But no matter how far he traveled, he was back by the time Pram began to get ready for bed. Before turning out the light, she would look from her bedroom window and see him at his tree, chasing ghost insects or rearranging the stars for his amusement.

It both comforted and worried Pram. She was not prepared for the day that Felix would lose interest in the living world and cross over completely.

"Have you thought about what you're going to say?" Clarence said, bringing Pram back into the world of the living, as he so often did.

"I'd like to ask her about crossing over," Pram said.

"She taught me a lot about the spirit world, but not how to help a ghost move on."

"I wouldn't think ghosts need help crossing over," Clarence said.

"Most don't, from what I've seen," Pram said. "Others have a harder time. One of the elders got himself trapped in the floorboards after he died. I could see his face in the wood grain, and he howled for days."

"That's awful," Clarence said. "What did you do?"

"That's just the thing," Pram said. "I didn't know what to do. One night I was lying in bed, listening to him howl, feeling sorry for him, and suddenly it got quiet and he was gone."

She hugged her chest to ward off the chill the memory brought. "I think he was afraid to go alone. I could talk to him, but I didn't know how to convince him it was safe to go on."

Neither of them spoke for a while after that. They had each begun to think of their own mothers and were wondering what it had been like for them to cross over, and why they didn't stay around long enough to say good-bye. At least tip a picture frame on the wall or flicker a light—something. To lose one's mother was to lose the beginning of one's life story.

The sun was melting into the horizon by the time they reached the county jail. Pram and Clarence stopped walking. They stood in a puddle of melted snow in the parking lot, staring at the yellow light coming from the wide windows.

The men inside wore dark blue uniforms and they were moving about like perfect wooden soldiers, Pram thought, with painted mouths and arched helmets. It didn't seem real to her that she was standing in front of the jail, and that she had followed Lady Savant yet again.

She was sure Lady Savant had the answers she was looking for, but the question was whether she'd be willing to share them. The only thing Pram knew about her for certain was that she was not to be trusted.

"Only one way to find out," she said, thinking aloud.

She balled her fists at her side and stepped forward.

"If you're looking for her, she isn't here," a voice said. Pram looked up and saw Adelaide sitting on the roof, her legs dangling over the edge, her skirt rustling on its own breeze not of the living world. "She's gone."

"Gone?" Pram asked.

Clarence looked up as well, but all he saw were stars beginning to emerge as the sky darkened. "Is someone up there?" he asked.

Adelaide jumped to her feet. "You've brought a living boy," she said excitedly.

"This is Clarence," Pram said. "He can't see you."

"I'm used to that." Adelaide sighed. "And if you've

come here looking for Lady Savant, she's gone. They've taken her away to a special sort of hospital."

"An asylum?" Pram asked, her heart sinking. She was thinking of the memory she'd seen of Lady Savant as a girl, restrained by doctors who meant to take her gift away from her. Lady Savant had done many cruel things, but it all began with that memory, that feeling of power-lessness. Lady Savant collected souls and became the master of her own asylum just so she could be stronger than she had been that day. And now she was back in another place just like it.

Adelaide nodded. She had no reason to be fond of Lady Savant, but she did have an awful lot of sympathy for the living. She had been a very compassionate child when she was alive.

"If Lady Savant is gone, what are you doing here?" Pram asked.

Adelaide twisted back and forth so that her skirt swirled against her legs. "I followed her here, and I didn't want to follow her where she was going, and I didn't want to go back, either. It feels weird in that building with nobody living in it. Nobody lights candles or breathes. It made me feel like I was dead."

Adelaide *was* dead, but Pram felt it would be rude to point that out now.

"So, after Lady Savant left, I just sort of stayed here,

watching the policemen come and go, listening to them talk to each other and turn on their sirens. It makes me feel safe."

Pram was beginning to feel pity for Adelaide. She was a ghost, and as such she was safe wherever she went. She could hop from the tops of buildings and sail in the sky using clouds as her boat. But she was, and forever would be, a little girl, not very much younger than Pram. And little girls need things like candlelight and people for company.

Pram thought about inviting Adelaide to follow her back to the two-hundred-year-old colonial house. It was cozy and safe, and she could even play with Felix if he wasn't being a grump.

But that didn't seem like a proper solution. Adelaide would not be truly happy to go on haunting this world. She wasn't like Felix, who had no desire to remember who he had been when he was alive, or how he died. Now that she remembered her family, it seemed that she should be getting back to them.

"Adelaide," Pram said, "maybe it's time for you to move on."

Being Pram's friend had taught Clarence to listen for things he could not hear. He didn't see Adelaide, and he didn't know what she was saying, but he thought he could feel her presence. Just slightly. There was a difference in the air where a ghost stood. There was a change in Pram as well; her eyes dilated and her face was concentrated.

When Pram told the ghost it might be time to move on, Clarence could feel fear just then. He could taste it like copper and dirt on his lips.

Pram looked at him. "I'm sorry," she said. "I don't mean to ignore you."

"No," Clarence said. "What you're doing is important. Maybe Lady Savant wasn't the only one who could teach you how to help a spirit move on. Maybe Adelaide can teach you."

Pram paused. Then she said, "Adelaide says she doesn't know how to move on. She says that she's tried before and it hasn't felt right."

"Maybe you can teach each other, then," Clarence suggested.

Pram turned to look at Adelaide again and blinked. "She's gone."

"Gone as in she moved on?" Clarence asked.

"I don't think so," Pram said. "I think we frightened her."

CHAPTER
28

After dinner, Pram spent the evening with the elders, playing a game whose rules they made up as they went along. They had an old game board whose pieces were missing, and they used cough drops and caramels as pawns. The game didn't follow any logical set of rules, as was the case with most things the elders did, but Pram had fun anyway.

She very much liked the elders. They accepted her and did not ask many questions. They lived in their own worlds of make-believe. They did not care about dirty dishes or clean laundry or which bills needed to be paid, and they were not ghosts who might have needed her help. They were a warm, pleasant in-between, neither living nor dead.

One of the elders—Mrs. Marson—pinched Pram's cheek and said, "I've won. I've won this game."

Pram smiled. "You have," she said. It wasn't a game that made sense, and that was the best thing about it.

"Shall we have a rematch?" Mrs. Marson asked. Her eyes were very wide and dark, and Pram imagined that her eyes had looked that way when she was a child.

"No more games for Pram," Aunt Nan said. "It's time for her to go to bed."

Pram went upstairs, and as she got ready for bed, she looked through her bedroom window and saw Felix climbing his tree.

She thought about Mr. Hesterson, whose spirit had been trapped in the floorboards after he died. She had been very young when it happened, and it was around the time she'd begun talking to Felix. It had frightened her, and the aunts gave her strange looks when she skipped over the floorboards on her way upstairs. She had wanted terribly to help him.

And, as Pram was finding it difficult to sleep, eventually she thought about Finley, whose forgetfulness gave him solace, and Adelaide, who seemed very lonely. Pram wanted to help Adelaide the way she had wanted to help Mr. Hesterson. She was a bit older now, and she had visited the spirit world. That surely meant something.

When morning came, Pram had slept very little. She

opened her eyes at least an hour before her aunts would call upstairs for her to get ready for school. Even the elders were still sleeping, and the house was silent.

Pram was restless. During what little time she had slept, she dreamed of Lady Savant being driven to the very sort of place she feared the most. And she dreamed of Lady Savant when she was a girl named Claudette. If only she'd had people like Aunt Dee and Aunt Nan and Felix to love her, she might have used her gift for good things, Pram thought. She might be happy now.

I'll only do good things, Pram thought. She would learn to help spirits move on, and she would deliver their messages if they asked her to.

She stood at her bedroom window and watched Felix pace from the pond to the street and back again, as though he was working up the courage to go on another adventure.

"You care for him a lot, don't you?" a voice said.

Pram turned to find Adelaide sitting on her desk.

"His name is Felix," Pram said. "He was my first friend."

Adelaide stood. She brushed her fingers over Pram's things—sharpened pencils lined neatly beside a stack of papers, and a ceramic bluebird with a money slot in its back. "I've been thinking about what you said: that it's time for me to move on."

"Have you tried again?" Pram asked.

"Whenever I try, I feel myself getting stuck," Adelaide said. "I almost got trapped in the shards of a broken vase the last time. I close my eyes, and I'm standing in front of a hallway, but when I try to walk down it, it's too long and I lose track of which direction I'm supposed to go down."

"I could try to go with you," Pram said. The words came out before fear stopped them.

"How?" Adelaide said.

"Lady Savant showed me how to enter the memories of people who had died. Maybe I can enter your memory of the hallway and you could meet me there."

Adelaide looked hopeful. "If you died, too, you could move on with me."

"I'd like to live if I can help it," Pram said. "But I can try to see you through."

"Okay," Adelaide said.

All I have to do is want it, Pram thought. *Anything I want is mine.*

Her bedroom disappeared.

CHAPTER
29

Adelaide's memories were a kaleidoscope, each image incomplete but bright and moving too fast to be caught.

Pram focused on getting her feet to touch ground.

The memories hummed and then went quiet, like an audience as the curtains began to open.

"Is this the hallway you saw?" Pram asked as Adelaide stepped beside her.

It wasn't a hallway so much as the notion of a hallway. They were nowhere in the living world. There were no real floors or walls, but it did seem to be a hallway, although one that Pram would have a hard time explaining to anyone in the living world.

"Yes," Adelaide said. She was trying to sound brave, but Pram could see that she was frightened.

Pram took Adelaide's hand, and they began walking in a direction they hoped was forward.

The sound of typewriter keys began to tap, from one of Adelaide's memories. Adelaide skipped to the sound of them. It seemed to make her calm down.

But then another sound arose from a different memory—a loud splash. Even Pram could feel the memory of water filling up her mouth and nose. A scream nobody could hear.

Adelaide froze. The memory was in their way, and she couldn't bring herself to push through it. "This is the part where I die," she said. "I'd fallen into the ravine. I was trying to collect sparkly rocks and I fell in. Nobody could hear me."

"It's over now," Pram said. "It's only a memory. It can't hurt you."

Adelaide shook her head. "I'm never going to see my parents again. I'm going to drown."

"You will see them again," Pram insisted. "They're right on the other side of the water. They've surely been waiting a long time for you."

Adelaide whimpered. Her hair was wet now, her clothes muddy. She opened her fist, and it was full of small, sparkling rocks.

She looked at Pram. "Will you come with me?"

Pram could taste the dirt in the water. She could feel

her body in the living world beginning to drown, as that was Adelaide's last living memory. "I can't," she said. "It isn't my time to go; it's yours. But I'll wait right here and I'll help you if you get stuck."

Adelaide's feet were in a puddle that dripped from her clothes. She shivered from the cold of it, and her teeth chattered, and for a moment she was a living girl again. A living girl who was just about to die.

"Hold your breath," Pram said. "It'll be over quick."

Adelaide took a deep breath.

And then she was gone.

Pram remained in place for as long as she could, in case Adelaide needed her help. But Adelaide didn't return. The water, and the memory of water, disappeared.

CHAPTER 30

After school, Clarence and Pram walked to the library.

"What are we trying to find?" Clarence asked.

Pram opened a drawer in the card catalog. "Jacob Pierce," she said. "He was Adelaide's father. She said he was writing a novel when she died."

Clarence watched her comb through the cards. "What was it like being in the spirit world?"

"I wasn't there for very long," Pram said. "It was scary at first, and then the longer I stayed, the less scary it felt. And I had to remind myself that I mustn't get complacent. I still had living left to do."

"I don't know how you're so brave," Clarence said. "Death scares most people."

"Death isn't a punishment," Pram said, repeating what Finley had told her. "It's just what comes next."

Clarence smiled at Pram while she was too busy looking through cards to notice. A girl who lived right on the verge of death had been the one to make him love life again.

"Oh!" Pram said. "I think I found it. 'Pierce comma *J*.'"

They roamed the aisle until they found it, and Clarence stood on tiptoes to retrieve the thick book with the green spine. "*'The Third Bell*,'" he read aloud, and flipped through it. "It's over five hundred pages."

Pram looked over his shoulder and turned to the front pages. "It was published forty-three years ago," she said.

"So Adelaide had been haunting that place for all those years," Clarence said. "Wow."

"Time is different in the spirit world," Pram said. "It's like it doesn't pass at all. The sky changes colors as the hours go on, but you hardly even notice. And you can just forget anything you don't want to hold on to."

She knew what Clarence was thinking. "Your mother will remember you," she told him. "Just like you can let unpleasant things go, you hold on that much tighter to the things you love."

"You think so?" he asked.

"I really do," Pram said. "While Lady Savant held me captive, and I was beginning to forget the important things, thinking of you always reminded me who I was."

His cheeks burned pink.

"It's scary to think that she was powerful enough to steal memories like that," he said.

"She wanted me to get stronger before she tried to take my soul," Pram said. "I wonder if I would have been anywhere near as powerful as she was."

"It wouldn't matter if you were," Clarence said. "You could grow up to be ten times more powerful than she was, and you still wouldn't go around stealing memories, or tricking anyone into telling you their secrets."

"What happened to her was terrible," Pram said. "It could have happened to me."

"I would never let it," Clarence said. "Neither would your aunts. And besides, if you feel like you're forgetting who you are, I'll be sure to remind you."

"Even twenty years from now?" Pram asked.

"Even fifty years from now," Clarence said. He could swear he heard Felix's voice telling him, "You'd better." His cheeks were turning pink again. He cleared his throat. "Do you want to check out this book?"

Pram took the book from him and read a bit from some pages, considering.

"No," she said. "It seems like something I'll understand better when I'm older." Pram suspected there were a great many things she would understand better when she was older. "Let's come back for it in a few years."

Acknowledgments

A couple of years back, after Thanksgiving dinner with my family, I sat on the kitchen floor with my nine-year-old cousin, drawing silly pictures. She asked me if I was writing anything new. At the time, I was dragging my feet with an early draft of this story, but my own uncertainty kept it on the back burner. I had never attempted to write for younger readers and wasn't sure I could pull it off. Seeing this as an opportunity to test the waters, I told her, "I do have a story about a girl whose best friend is a ghost."

As I told my story, she began to draw the things I described. From then on, she asked me about Pram and her ghost whenever we spoke. It was her enthusiasm that made me believe this story might have a place in the hearts of younger readers, which gave me the courage to finish it. For that, I owe a huge thank-you to my cousin Riley Victoria Fallon. Her insights and knowledge are vastly beyond her years, and someday the literary community and the world will know her name.

As always, a huge thank-you goes to my parents and my huge extended family, for indulging me with their support and love.

Thank you to the greatest support system in the world: Beth Revis, Laura Bickle, and Aimée Carter for encouraging me. And to Tahereh Mafi, who sent all those caps lock–addled e-mails that were so fun to receive as she read an early draft of this story. And a special thank-you to Aprilynne Pike and her daughter Audrey for offering their insights. You guys are truly the best.

Thanks, as always, to my agent, Barbara Poelle, whose love for this story got me through the dark patches of writing it. And to my brilliant editor, Cat Onder, for believing in Pram's journey and offering such fantastic insights. Huge thank-you to Donna Mark, Amanda Bartlett, and Kevin Keele for creating a cover that captures Pram's spirit and her friendship with Felix better than I could have imagined. Thank you to the entire team at Bloomsbury for allowing me to be a part of the process, from the cover to the title and all the pages therein. What a rare and wonderful journey this story has been.

Lionel and Marybeth are best friends in a world that has forgotten about them. So when a mysterious blue spirit possesses Marybeth—and starts to take control—they know they must stop it before the real Marybeth fades away forever.

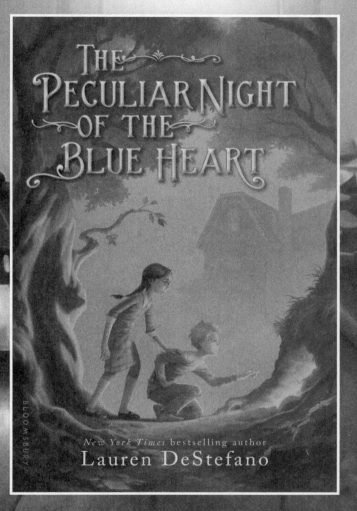

THE PECULIAR NIGHT OF THE BLUE HEART

New York Times bestselling author
Lauren DeStefano

BLOOMSBURY

Don't miss *New York Times* bestselling author
Lauren DeStefano's haunting tale of friendship,
love . . . and what lies beyond.

*L*ionel was a wild boy. Sometimes he forgot he was a boy at all. He growled and purred, and fell asleep curled beneath the table during breakfast.

Mrs. Mannerd was always exasperated with Lionel, but she had seven other children to mind, and some days it was easier to serve him his porridge under the table than it was to make him use a chair.

Lionel might have been useful if only he'd been cooperative. When he talked to the chickens, they would lay eggs, but he would not dare steal them from the roosts. He was so patient and so still and so endearing that he could lure a wild rabbit into his hands, but he would not allow Mr. Porter, the butcher, to skin it for supper. One afternoon he walked into the barn just as Mr. Porter was about to take an ax to the Thanksgiving turkey, and he screamed and caused such a ruckus that the turkey was spooked and took off running, and feeble old Mr. Porter had to chase it around the barn with his bad back and his ax in one hand, all as Lionel shouted, "Run, run!" and tried to set the turkey free.

It had been a delicious turkey supper, but Lionel spent the whole meal sobbing in the darkness of the stairwell, blowing his nose on the good napkins with the embroidered fleurs-de-lis that the late Ms. Gillingham had imported from France (God rest her soul).

Everyone in the house agreed that the boy was strange, except for Marybeth. Marybeth could often be found following Lionel, and she always offered him some of the pralines that her second cousin sent for the holidays.

Marybeth was a very normal girl, with dark hair that she wore braided into pigtails, and round spectacles with red metal rims. She always washed her face and brushed her teeth without being asked, and what she wanted with a boy like Lionel was perplexing to everyone in the house.

Mrs. Mannerd hoped that some of Marybeth's graces would rub off on the boy. Marybeth was nine and Lionel was nine and three-quarters, but she was at least five years wiser—or so Mrs. Mannerd liked to say.

But Marybeth hoped she wasn't an influence on Lionel; she quite liked him the way he was: clever and brave, as though he could never be harmed simply because it never occurred to him.

Before she followed him outside that morning, Marybeth snuck two of Mrs. Mannerd's coconut cookies into her dress pockets and ran through the screen door in the kitchen. Lionel was already several yards ahead, and she hurried to catch up to him, her braids bouncing against her shoulders. "Where are you going?" she asked him.

It was a question Lionel heard often. He never sat still and he was always going somewhere, and he was always gone for a long time. He was very good at not answering. He would yawn or bite into an apple or howl like a wolf. But he liked Marybeth; she never scolded him or stole his pillow or told him to eat his stew. So he gave her a straight answer. "I'm going to make friends with a fox I saw last week."

"Is it one of Mrs. Rustycoat's babies?" Marybeth asked. Mrs. Rustycoat was the name of a fox they'd found last spring. She wouldn't come close while Marybeth was in tow, but Lionel told her that when he was alone, Mrs. Rustycoat came and ate blueberries from his hand. He said she was so aloof and cautious because she had a litter somewhere.

"It wasn't one of hers," Lionel said. "It had a blue coat."

"Can foxes be blue?" Marybeth asked.

"I've never heard of it," Lionel said. "But I know what I saw. It stood on its hind legs and looked at me and then ran into a shrub."

"Did you look it up in the encyclopedia?" Marybeth asked.

"Mrs. Mannerd says I'm banned from the encyclopedias for a week."

"That's the silliest thing I've ever heard."

"She said they give me wild ideas."

Mrs. Mannerd was an adult, and had been one for a long time. So long, in fact, that the children suspected she had no memory of being a child herself. Her hair was gray and she was very tall. She was afraid of children with wild ideas. She said that she'd been caring for orphans for forty years and she had seen all kinds of children—good ones and mean ones and smart ones and dull ones—but she had never under all her stars had a child like Lionel. She once said that Lionel must have been born in a barn, and Marybeth politely pointed out that Jesus had been born in a barn, and Mrs. Mannerd didn't have anything to say to that except, "Finish your carrots, Marybeth."

Lionel had smiled at her from across the table. Only for a moment, though, and then he dipped his head. He didn't like for the other children to know what he was thinking.

He was in good spirits now. He stepped into the woods, as light on his feet as a ghost. Marybeth stayed close behind him and tried not to make too much noise. She looked over her shoulder just once, to see how far they'd gone from the little red house where Mrs. Mannerd would be collecting the laundry from the hampers right about now, muttering about things the children left in their pockets. The older ones would be in their rooms studying their French and their cursive, no doubt envious of Marybeth and Lionel, who were the only children young enough to be allowed to squander their Saturday mornings outside.

Not long ago, there had been another child their age, a little girl with long hair and eyes the same color as when the daylight hits the sea. She was extremely polite and curtsied when she said hello. She was adopted by a young couple with kind eyes and creased clothes, and once she was gone, Mrs. Mannerd told the children, "You see what happens when you behave?"

There were infants sometimes as well. They came and went, each one identical to the one before it. Mrs. Mannerd didn't like infants. They always needed something, and they couldn't help out around the house. But they were adopted off soon enough. Babies were preferred by the barren. Best to shape them from the beginning, rather than taking an older child and dealing with who they've already become.

Lionel was certain that nobody would ever adopt him. That suited him just fine. As soon as he was old enough, he would live in the woods and be a wild thing, and he would never eat porridge again.

"Stop," he said, and held out his arms. When the leaves ceased to crunch under Marybeth's scuffed black boots, he listened. The animal was nearby. He could feel its pulse in the air, like the rumble of a train getting closer.

He crouched low, and then he began to crawl.

Marybeth stood still, holding her breath for as long as she could stand just to be quiet.

Finally she said, "It won't come out because I'm here."

Lionel stood. His eyes were distant, and at first Marybeth didn't think he'd heard her, but then he said, "Maybe."

"I can go inside."

"I don't want you to go," Lionel said. He wasn't looking at her, and he gnawed on his lip pensively as he considered the hiding animal, unaware of how his words had touched her. Marybeth, like the other children in the house, was unaccustomed to being told she was wanted.

"Come out, you stubborn thing," Lionel said. "Mr. Porter and the older ones aren't here. It's just us."

"Maybe it's best that it's scared, whatever it is," Marybeth said. "No animal would become supper if it knew to stay away from humans."

"We aren't humans," Lionel said. "We're Lionel and Marybeth."

Sometimes, for just a moment, Marybeth stood on the very edge of his world, and through the shadows she could almost see what he was thinking.

"Come on," she said. "We can go to the river and talk to the fish. They always come to you."

"All right," Lionel said, quite frustrated with the blue creature, who could not, it seemed, know the difference between an ordinary human and Marybeth. He began to suspect he had overestimated the thing's intelligence.

They spent the rest of the morning making faces at the fish and chasing each other, giggling as they caught each other between the trees until Mrs. Mannerd called them to their chores, and they ran to her voice.

That evening, after dinner, Lionel slipped outside as the older ones argued over who got to take the first bath while there was still plenty of hot water.

Mrs. Mannerd knew that Lionel had gone because he'd left the storm door open, and the wind made it flutter against the frame.

She also knew that going after him would prove futile. He was quick as a fox, and he liked to climb. She lost her breath chasing after him, always to no end.

Marybeth, however, was never any trouble to find. She was sitting at the empty table, her posture ever straight as she read from a cover-worn book she'd checked out of the library.

"Do you know where Lionel's gone off to?" Mrs. Mannerd said.

"To feed the foxes, maybe," Marybeth offered. "He had berries in his pocket."

So that was why the blueberries kept disappearing, Mrs. Mannerd thought.

Marybeth closed her book. "I can find him."

"Don't be too long. The sun's going down."

Of all the children in the house, Marybeth was the only one to ever do as she was told, and without complaint, no less. She didn't even need to be reminded to put on her coat before she opened the door.

When Marybeth stepped outside, she was greeted by a gust of cool autumn wind. This was the time of year when Lionel was more prone to disappear. After most of the birds had abandoned their nests in preparation for the winter, he turned his focus to the foxes and rabbits, and left offerings to the coyotes in the hopes of charming them as well.

She knew better than to call out to him. Her voice would only startle whatever small creature he was trying to allure.

She was no expert tracker; she wasn't deft or silent. But she did know Lionel, and she could see the subtle traces that he left on his way out of the house. For starters, he never stepped in the soft earth like the kind that had formed after yesterday's rain. Soft earth left footprints. He would hop over that and tread only in the grass.

Marybeth looked for the grass that was slightly bent. There was an empty patch where she remembered seeing some clovers earlier. They were gone now, which meant that Lionel had plucked them.

He would feed them to the rabbits, she thought. Along with the bits of bark that were missing from a nearby tree.

Moving as quietly as she could, she ascended into the tree line and made her way to the warren.

Sure enough, she found Lionel lying on his stomach, looking into a mossy opening beside a giant tree. He didn't look at Marybeth, but she saw his ears prick up. He was being a rabbit himself just then.

She took a step toward him.

"Quiet," he whispered, and made room for her beside him.

Marybeth lowered herself onto the ground, breathing as quietly as she could.

Lionel looked at her, and only she would have been able to recognize the smile in his eyes, on his face that was otherwise firm with concentration. "There's a fat mother rabbit in there," he said. His voice sounded just like the wind, his words barely audible. "She's shy, but she can't resist the clovers. Give me your hand."

Marybeth held out her hand, watching curiously as he filled her palm with rumpled clovers.

"Hold it up by the entrance," he said, nodding to the small cavern. "Go on."

Marybeth did as he instructed with a sense of caution. Lionel sometimes tried to include her in his endeavors with wild creatures, but she lacked his natural magic. She always ended up scaring the poor things away.

For several seconds, nothing happened. It was beginning to get dark, and soon Mrs. Mannerd would grow cross with them.

"Lionel—"

"Shh. Shh. Look."

Marybeth sensed the rabbit before she saw it. It peeked its gray-brown head from its warren and twitched its nose against her fingertip. Marybeth felt a chill and did her best not to giggle.

Bit by bit, the rabbit came out into view. It really was

a chubby thing, and it went for the clovers in Marybeth's palm. It looked at her with its nervous black eyes as it chewed.

Lionel talked softly to it, murmuring sweet things mothers said to sleeping babies—or so Marybeth would imagine—and stroking its cheek with his knuckle.

A sharp gust of wind pushed across the sky, rattling the bare branches and fallen leaves. The rabbit's ear twitched, and it hopped back into hiding.

Marybeth burst into giggles and rolled onto her side. "I don't think she liked me very much."

"Sure she did," Lionel said. "It's taken all week for me to get her to come out." A smile was beginning to creep onto his serious features. Marybeth plucked a blade of grass from his unruly hair.

She was the only one he would allow to do such a thing. When Mrs. Mannerd attempted to comb his hair, he hissed. *Be reasonable!* Mrs. Mannerd would cry, which of course only made him less reasonable. But Marybeth never told him what to do. She never tried to tame him, not even when she didn't understand why he behaved the way that he did. She merely cared for him, the way that he cared for the rabbits. The way a mother bird guarded her nest.

"What did you do with the berries you took?" she asked.

"I left them by the river. I'm sure I saw the blue fox go there."

Marybeth stared at the bit of clovers still in her palm. It was a simple-enough thing, a clover; people stepped over them on their way to grander things. But she knew that it was the greatest thing Lionel had to offer her. It was an invitation into his peculiar world.

From far away, they heard the storm door open.

"Children!" Mrs. Mannerd called.

Marybeth cringed. "I was supposed to find you and bring you back inside." She stood and held out her hands. He took them, and she pulled him to his feet.

The smile was still lingering on his face, and it grew. "Race you back."

He took off running before she could answer.

"Lionel!"

He held an unfair advantage, and he knew it. He was barefoot while she wore stiff leather shoes that were secondhand and a size too small. And when he had a mind to be, he was the wind itself, flying over the surface of the earth, impossible to catch.

But when he reached the side of the little red house, he waited for her. That was the thing that made him human again.

The wind and rain picked up late that night. The older ones did not notice storms, and they slept on.

Marybeth shared a bedroom with three older girls, and she slept on the rickety top bunk beside the window that overlooked the woods. There was a maple tree that grew beside the house, and its branches would rap on the glass when it was especially windy, as though it wanted to wake her and show her something.

Only there was never anything out there to see. Marybeth rubbed the sleep from her eyes and squinted through the blur of her nearsighted vision.

She was just falling back to sleep when she saw it: a flicker of blue.

She sat upright immediately, unsure if she had dreamed it. She reached for her spectacles, hanging from a nail in the wall above her pillow.

The edges of the swaying trees came into focus. When the branches moved just so, she saw it again, a flash of blue.

She descended the ladder from her bed, minding the missing rung that had broken off before she came to live there.

There were no windows in the upstairs hallway, and without so much as the moonlight to guide her, Marybeth walked with her hand along the wall to make her way.

The door to the boys' room was slightly ajar. Marybeth could hear the older ones snoring.

"Lionel," she whispered. His bed was farthest from the door, in a corner where the ceiling leaked when it rained. He kept a galvanized bucket at the foot of his bed, and Marybeth could hear the *plunk, plunk, plunk* of water falling into it. "Lionel!"

One of the older ones stopped snoring. He sat up, his silhouette all black against a flash of lightning that brightened the window.

"I was dreaming that I was a king, and then you woke me," he told her. "If I'm not still king when I go back to sleep, I'll hang you by your toes."

He might do it, Marybeth knew. She'd been locked

in closets and framed for the older ones' offenses, so that she'd be punished with their chores. The older ones made a game of tormenting Marybeth and Lionel, but Marybeth especially, because she was easier to catch and too timid to defend herself.

"Beat it," the older one said, and Marybeth shrank away from the doorway. If she wanted to look for the blue creature, she would have to go alone and tell Lionel about it in the morning.

She made her way down the stairs, knowing precisely which ones to avoid because they creaked, and took the lantern from the hall closet and struck a match to light the candle. After that, she grabbed her yellow rain slicker from its hook by the door. She wriggled her feet into her rain boots, which were a size too large and beginning to come apart from their soles. They were older than Marybeth herself and had been worn by every child to live in this house before her.

The cold wind filled the house as she opened the door, splattering the floorboards with rain. Marybeth moved quickly, pulling the door shut tight behind her and hoping the sound wouldn't wake Mrs. Mannerd in her bed.

Lauren DeStefano is the *New York Times* and *USA Today* bestselling author of *A Curious Tale of the In-Between*; *The Peculiar Night of the Blue Heart*; the Internment Chronicles; and the Chemical Garden trilogy, which includes *Wither*, *Fever*, and *Sever*. She earned her BA in English with a concentration in creative writing from Albertus Magnus College in Connecticut.

www.laurendestefano.com
www.laurendestefano.tumblr.com
@LaurenDeStefano